The ShadowTracks® Collection

ShadowTracks

—Finding A Place For The Love—

by

Mimi Halo

Illustrations by Randy Perdew

Plickity Plunk™ Press

Special Thanks
to all who contributed
to the evolution
of this heartfelt tale

International Standard Book Number: 0-9670896-1-1
Library of Congress Catalog Card Number: 99-90220

FIRST EDITION
Printed in the United States of America by Morris Publishing

Published The United States of America by

Plickity Plunk™ Press
P.O. Box 37
Caliente, CA 93518

website: http://www.plickityplunk.com

To Douglas,
who found me
in the moonlight...
and gave my mountains
a name

A 'shadowtrack'
is an impression on the moment,
whether it shows itself
in a raindrop's ripple on the pond,
or in the shade of a tree,
or in a tender remembering

—CONTENTS—

"Hark, dear meadow," called the crow
as he soared high above the rolling hills
and spotted woods
of birch and maple, hickory and oak.

"I carry word from the North.
Prepare...for winter brings a flurry of snow.

I see the frost has done well to ready the ground,
weaving coverlets of ice crystals all around,
but there's a patch down by the mill
that needs a good mend.
I know how the first snow can tickle
a bare meadow, my friend..."

And it was as the crow told.
There was a great snow. But rest assured, quite a few more than one of those flurries has made this winter coat.

Aaah... What a night the crisp air of winter brings to this snow-covered mountainside meadow, trimmed in moonlit silhouettes of pines and old weathered split rail fencing.

There'll be clover growing here in the spring, but for now, most everything is sleeping. Flowers hidden within all the tiny seeds that were sprinkled about last season by the wind and the birds and the bees, lay quietly dreaming of what they'll be—safely tucked beneath the beds of fallen leaves.

Occasionally there's a visit from some raindrop friends or the snow. Father Sun keeps them warm, and the moon tells them stories only those of the meadow would know.

All the stars, arched across the sky, forever twinkle lullabies to help pass the time. They couldn't be brighter tonight. It looks like it's going to snow again soon, too, with that halo around the moon.

Mmmmm... Smell the hickory burning? Reminds me of Christmas. It'll be here in a few days. I wonder what the Christmas trees will have to say. For some it means the end of being green, but that's okay—in a way. Endings bring beginnings, and beginnings bring the spring.

See the lights down there in the valley, dancing in reds and greens and whites. It's the wind whispering through the trees, nudging snowflakes and other little things on with their journeys.

We all need the love of a nudge every once in awhile. It helps us to get unstuck. For even the tiniest of things has a reason for being, and its journey can seem just as rough.

I know, for I am this meadow and the foothills beyond. As far as you can see, down to the jagged rocky beach, that is me; and all who live here are the children of my dreams. I feel the wishes and the pains and the passing of the smallest of precious things: the falling petals of a flower, the dew when it meets the morning sun, the pond's ripple from the tickle of a feisty snowflake's plunge.

My clothes are a collection of many weights and weaves, from the elm who's grown too weak to make another leaf to the plickity-plunks of the orchard's overbearing apple tree—not to mention the pitter-patter of a trillion busy feet.

The children of the meadow follow their dreams. Some return with every spring. Some go on to be other things. In a trail of echoes and shadows can be seen, the legacy of journeys different becomings can bring.

For only in living the life of a particular seed, does a little soul really know how it feels to be a tree. And only by sharing the water and wind with the sun, does one of the meadow begin to value its love.

—ShadowTracks—

Plickity Plunk

PART I

One

Tender Beginnings ~

So begins this story as I feel a tender tug...

plickity plunk. . .plunk

Ah... the drop of an acorn nut.

He should have fallen long before now, and with the snow, it'll be hard to find a place underground. But that's what you get for being afraid of heights. Even birds have to make the same scarey first flight.

The acorn's name is Jymee (shy-me). He's inside asleep, in a sort of dream weave in between being things even though he's a seed. He temporarily misplaced the fact that he decided to be a tree.

With the coming of day, a passing squirrel picked Jymee up and scurried away, down across the brook and over a stonewall where, in a scare, the acorn got dropped into a pillow of snow—only that night, to get stepped on,

~Ouch?#*! ~

...when a big hoof came along.

Jymee wasn't broken, just buried til the thaw. If it weren't for that little bit of help, he could have been a nut for a long long time. Seedlings don't grow well in the snow. It's too cold.

"Brrr... I'm cold," was heard in an echo from down below.

Jymee will be fine. The inside of his shell is lined.

Spring, as usual, came in an unpredictable way: cold then warm, snow then rain, but it got here, and that's okay.

The warmth woke and softened the land, as one by one, timid green beginnings are coaxed to uncurl and stand. It had been some time since they'd seen the sun shine. It's bright! —Or felt the breeze on their leaves. The world beneath is dark and compact. You don't always know where you're growing, but it feels better than where you've been at.

Spring's thaw softened Jymee's shell, as water seeped in and he began to swell.

With a stretch and a crack appeared a root. And with another stretch and a crack, came to curious attention...his shoot.

~It's all mushy out here~ Jymee thought, as he began to explore the soft spring slush. ~Maybe I'm asleep~

WOOZH...

WOOZH....

WOOZH....

...came from something wushing down beneath.

WOOZH...

WOOZH....

WOOZH....

~That wushing wasn't me~ Jymee realized as the wushing took it's leave.

Underground it's black. Nothing moves fast.

With every stretch, Jymee grew an inch or two—until, in one stretch,

Clunk!?

"Ow *#?!"

...he bumped into something that

Boo'D!

"Who! Who's there!?" clamored a crusty old voice in the dark.

"I'm...not really sure," Jymee timidly remarked.

"Well you can't just go bumping around. You gave me a scare," the voice fussed and fidgeted. "I got fruit grow'n. Now I'm not sure who's hang'n where!"

"Fruit?" Jymee timidly inquired.

"Yeller-red stripe'd fruit. I'm not all root, you know. I do have another side," the gnarly old root replied. This is just the part that lives in the dark. I got a tree grow'n in the light."

"A tree?"

"A reflection, so to speak. Up there they'd probably call this here root a branch and maybe this knot a leaf, but down here I'm all root. Plain and simple. The part that lives underneath. You'll see."

"I will?" Jymee questioned, bewildered at the thought.

"That's what see-dlings do! Only half of you is supposed to be root," Jymee learned as he felt an unexpected tickle to the tip of his tap.

"Oh?!"

"Yep, feels like baby oak." said the grandfather root. "Know any of them folk?"

"No," Jymee couldn't recall.

"Well, you will, when you break through."

"But... then what'll I do?" Jymee asked.

"Be a green grow'n shoot for awhile, unless you get chewed."

"Chewed?" Jymee questioned.

"There's all kinds of creepy crawly stuff that'll want to eat you."

"Eat—me?" Jymee feared.

"Just keep thinking tree," the root assured him, "You'll be okay. But you gotta change direction. You're grow'n the wrong way."

"The wrong way?"

"You gotta grow up!"

"Up?"

"Didn't you get any kind of directions with that nut?" the root huffed. "Oh, no sense mak'n a fuss. But right now you're sitting under old Tinystones and he doesn't have any holes in his rocks."

"Tinystones?"

"He's the stonewall around these parts. So you're gonna have to curl back the way you came and then up. You'll start seeing twinkle-glows as you near the light."

"Twinkle-glows. All right," Jymee timidly replied, accepting his plight.

"Just don't turn up too close," the root advised. "I got fruit that roll."

"Oh."

"Now get grow'n before your tap builds up mold."

Jymee reluctantly curled back the way he came. It was cold and silent and blacker-than-black, not a world he felt like re-living again.

~ A nut ~ Jymee reflected, ~ he called me a nut. Why didn't I get any kind of directions for growing up? ~

With every inch, Jymee grew more and more confused. No direction felt like any direction, but growing was all he could do.

~ Peek-a-boo ~

~ Peek-a-boo ~ came in a soft playful echo from somewhere... Maybe up.

In a wink, Jymee saw a tiny twinkle, and then it was gone.

~ Maybe that was a twinkle-glow ~ Jymee thought, as he turned and grew in that blacker-than-black direction for awhile.

~ *Peek-a-boo... little nut-nut* ~ came in another twinkle that seemed to flicker and glow, soft snuggly feelings Jymee had always known.

~ *Remember me?* ~ the tiny twinkle echoed in a blush.

Jymee tried to recall the feeling, but somehow his treasure chest of memories must have been locked.

Sensing his puddle of misplaced-keepsakes, the twinkle sadly began to fad.

"Don't go away," Jymee pleaded, "I'm sure I'd remember if you could tell me the place. Where'd you come from? The light?"

It was too late. The twinkle had twinked out of sight.

Jymee held on to those warm snuggly feelings as he grew in that dark dark place, hoping to see the twinkle-glow again, but it never came.

His world took on an icey dampness, so cold he could barely move.

~ Wherever I'm growing is bending my shoot. ~
It was too late to change direction. He could only grow one way. So he grew and he grew until gradually, his bend turned into straight.

In a flush of tipsy-lightness, Jymee's very-most peak met the edge of dawn. It was so bright and light. He was glad his roots were there to hang on.

* ~dink~ *

* * ~dink~

"Ooooo... who are you?" Jymee giggled in a tickle, as little somethings dinked his shoot.

* ~dink~ *

* ~dink~ *

* * ~dink~

There were two, then there were three, but with every dink they melted away.

*

*

~ Where'd they go? ~ Jymee thought.

*

It was an April snow, just a brush to let the flowers know what it's like on the other side. It'd be gone by noontide. The ducks wouldn't have to fly.

With every inch of lightness, the darkness grew further away. Jymee found himself sprouting in mid-air. This was a very curious place.

In a yawn, his shoot uncurled a little green leaf, and soon a few more yawns made it three, floppy green leaves bouncing in the breeze.

Jymee didn't have much of a view. There was a stone wall, home to some ivy and moss and a salamander or two. It had been made years before from a collection of rocks, placed one upon the other, just high enough to inform a passerby of the land's divide between the woods and the lakeside.

Around Jymee too, were other green growing shoots, mostly taller than he; but Jymee had the sky: the blues and the greys, the sun and the clouds passing by... not to mention the birds and the butterflies... and the moon and the stars at night... and lots of croaks and gurgles and honks he couldn't identify.

It took til midsummer before Jymee reached blade peak height and that was mostly because the old grass had died.

Plickity Plunk

Occasionally, a mole or a squirrel would scurry by, and then there was an owl who'd catch mice at night. All Jymee could do was hope the owl wouldn't eat him too.

One day a beaver waddled on through and didn't even say excuse me when his tail flattened Jymee's shoot. Jymee recovered after he swallowed his pride.

Anyway, the fireflies were nice. Every now and then one would land on a leaf and blink, not really say anything; but it made Jymee feel like he had a friend. It was overwhelming to live in a jungle of so many things bigger than him.

Crickets were another thing. Their chirps might be nice to keep company a balmy night; but when you're tiny sized and one decides to hang out where you permanently reside, you have no choice but to listen.

ikit...

ikit...

ikit...

The cricket couldn't stop. Ikits were the greater part of his rendition.

By the time summer was through, Jymee had grown another inch or two. His leaves were a little chewed. He'd been rained on and sat on. It's not easy being a shoot.

Even a spider decided to weave a coverlet over his view. It was airy and see-through til the eve, when it would sink into a soppy wet blanket with the dew.

Fall brought changes from greens to browns and reds as the trees began to shed. Jymee noticed some changes too. The few floppy green leaves he tried so hard to preserve, started to shrivel up and turn brown.

~ What's happening to me? ~ Jymee feared.

They just hung down.

A soft sunset brought in the twilight, as Jymee watched a flock of geese in V-formation fly south across the sky, just as he'd watched another flock at noontide. Storm clouds were rolling in, and the wind began to stir the leaves. In a whisk,

Jymee's three were set free.

He frantically searched among the tumbling debris, trying to identify his lost little leaves.

"Where'd they go? Where'd they go?"

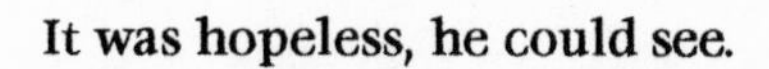

It was hopeless, he could see.

"Why? Why my leaves? Jymee saddened at the wind, feeling torn and empty inside. "Why?"

Too hurt, he turned his thoughts inward and sunk his heart down to his roots.

~ Those were a part of me. ~

At least it was peaceful down there. No wind to bother him.

The gustiness calmed, as the night went on, making room for a drizzle to meet the dawn. Jymee's spider coverlet was gone. The misty rain felt good on his tattered shoot.

Inklings of sun on the early morning dew, coaxed Jymee to turn up from down deep in his roots. He was a little tender to the day, not really sure why he was there in the first place.

Timidly he looked around. His world had changed. It was a little lighter and brighter. No more clinging things. In a funny way, it felt good to be free even though he'd lost his leaves. So did all the other trees—except for one maybe. It was still green and looked sort of fuzzy from where Jymee was standing.

There was some gurgling nearby.

noflo~nogwo~

~noflo~nogwo~

Jymee had heard it before, every once in a while.

As he stretched for a peek in that direction, over an old piece of curled bark, he saw glistening water trickling over clumps of rock and around mossy bends, carrying twigs and leaves in the same direction as had flown the geese.

In the crispness of the autumn morn, a forest butterfly, dressed in yellow and grey, danced about the water's banks, coming to rest on the stem of an overblown and dangling dandelion.

She just sat there, staring into the sky, parting her wings every once in awhile. Her mind seemed preoccupied.

Jymee overheard her speaking when the breeze blew her voice to him.

"Guess there's only me," the butterfly said. "Flowers went away. Lake said Frost will come tonight. I can't stay. Lake said say bye, til next time. Why? Why was I a caterpillar so long? Oh dear... So many eggs to leave behind. No time... No time..."

Jymee readied himself, standing brave and gallant to aid the lady fair. He looked a little torn and tattered, but...

"I, know I'm a little squished," he whispered," and out of shape. I lost my leaves yesterday, but I'm okay, I think. If you want, you can sit on me—for company, I mean."

"Ohhh???" came in a startled reply, as the butterfly fluttered and lifted up and off into the breeze.

"But, I..." Jymee tried to apologize.

She darted here and there, circling once and once again, hesitantly, and then suddenly seemed to vanish in the trees.

~Did I... say something... wrong?~ Jymee thought.

In all his confusion, Jymee wanted to go run away and hide too, but he was stuck as a tree. He didn't even have one single solitary leaf to hide beneath.

So there he stood, swaying in the breeze.

~She sat on that old bent-over stem~ he thought about the dandelion. ~Do I look worse than him?~

That night, while Jymee was sleeping under the moon half-full and a sky sprinkled with stars, a wisp of fairylikeness made a slow and lazy flight about the brookside, dipping down every once in awhile as if to kiss each who lived there good night.

In time, she came to Jymee, touching down.

~Bye...~ the butterfly whispered, as she turned to go, but something made her linger in a gentle flutter about his shoot.

~ You cared about me. Why? ~ she asked the sleeping seedling. ~ Why would you care about a butterfly? ~

The wind carried a chill that said she had to fly; but before she left, she drew close to Jymee and curled forward her tail, touching his shoot and tenderly laying an egg on his side.

~ Bye... ~

She disappeared into the night. And as the lake said, the dew became the frost. Jymee slept through the change, but our butterfly friend was too fragile.

Her name was Twink.

Two

Nibble ~

It got colder as the days passed through October. All the summer sounds were gone. An icey mist covered the wispy wayfarers of autumn as the ground hardened beneath the frost. The animals grew chubby with extra fur and the trees with extra bark. Even Jymee's shoot gradually turned from green to sapling gray, just in time to greet the first sprinkle of snowflakes. They stayed a day and then melted away, soon returning in a burst of wintry-white to blanket the December forest.

Jymee lost his view when snowflakes decided to drift over and cozy the stonewall too, but that was okay. It gave him plenty of time to think.

In the stillness of all that white, Jymee felt a snuggly fuzziness at his roots. It tickled a little, but it felt good too. ~Hm, I wonder who's playing with my roots~ Jymee thought. He was sure it had to be friendly, because it didn't bite.

One full-moon-bright and starry night, as all but the murmuring brook were craddled and quiet, a wave of sparkles and stardust lightly shimmered and danced across the snow-covered woods, playing in jingles on all the icicles and anything else that tingled.

* tingle *

jingle *

Buried in snowflakes, asleep with his dreams, Jymee found himself looking like a tree with one branch and some leaves; and there was a tall slender stem standing next to him. Over the wall, in the distance, off the tip of his branch, he could see a glimmering lake with an island... and there was this gnarly old tree with all these yellow-red stripe'd balls dangling. Jymee didn't want to blink. He wanted to hang on to the dream, but in the unexpected sound of a crackle-crunch, it left him anyway.

With another crackle-crunch, and a bend and a boing, from beneath the icey crust of winter, suddenly appeared Jymee in the twinkling twilight.

As he teeter-tottered to a standstill, Jymee caught sight of the big burly beaver who had just set him free, crackle-crunching his way downstream.

~noflo~nogwo~

~noflo~nogwo~

"And to think," Jymee reflected. "I used to be mad at him."

Hanging low in the sky, Jymee saw the same clump of stars that had been twinkling before the snowflakes arrived. He sure loved those sparkly things. Maybe it's because the sky's been around for lifetimes.

Jymee got buried in a few more blizzards before spring brought the thaw; but as he gradually uncovered, he discovered he'd grown a smidgen taller.

In a stretch to see over the wall, he found he was still an inch shy. Things don't grow that fast in the wintertime.

Looking around and down, Jymee noticed a twig sticking out of the snow.

~ Who's that? ~ he gasped.

With a little more melting, its beginning was shown.

"That's coming from me!?" he discovered.

And with the last of the melt, "Have I got two?"

Well, it was only a starter, barely enough to be considered a branch, but in time it would be one.

~ All these green spots... I must be sick ~ Jymee feared.

They were only buds, the sun tried to assure him; but Jymee was too busy being scared—that was until one tiny shiny green leaf happily appeared.

It was a strange and wonderful day. Where he had been one, now he was three: a trunk and two branches. Suddenly Jymee felt like a tree. He had some balance, finally. He was so proud, he could hardly stand still.

"You all are gonna have to go around me from now on. I'm a permanent resident of this here ground!"

A few weeks later, as Jymee was gloating over his leaves, he noticed this tiny green beginning within less than two feet. It made some soft timid sounds in its attempt to uncurl from the ground. Jymee remembered the feeling well.

"I wish I could help," he tenderly told the tiny being.

"You did," murmurred the little green shoot in a stretch, as she straightened herself.

"I did?"

"All winter long, " replied the tiny green beginning as she looked around at all the yellows and blues and greens and purples and pinks of spring. "Is this really spring?" she whispered in awe, hardly believing all she saw.

"Did you say all winter long?" Jymee asked.

"I've been snuggled at your roots," the shoot giggled, as Jymee felt a tickle too.

"So you're the fuzzy feeling," Jymee figured.

"Oh, my roots... I guess they tickle. I'm sorry."

"Please don't be," Jymee was quick to insist. "It felt... I mean, it feels kind of nice, actually."

"I'm a lady slipper," she bashfully confessed, "or at least that's what I'll be. I had to stay down below until I was strong enough to be up here in the light with other things."

~noflo~nogwo~

~noflo~nogwo~

The little shoot suddenly perked to attention as the spring air silenced to the gurgling brook.

"Do I hear gurgles?" the little shoot asked.

"Gurgles? Why yes," Jymee said.

"Do they sparkle ?"

"Sometimes."

"And are there clumps of fuzzy green moss?"

"I think I see some," Jymee guessed.

"And do twigs and leaves ride atop?"

"Lots! I don't know where they're going, but the water never stops."

That's Seamore!" the little shoot delighted. "Oh, I'm so glad he's here. If I could only be a little taller."

"You'll get there," Jymee assured her.

Plickity Plunk

"I know Seamore from underneath," she explained. "He told me about spring. And here it is! Funny thing. He's a part of the lake that likes to live in the woods. I always wished I'd green by him. This is perfect!"

"So, is that how you found me?" Jymee marveled of this cheerful burst of green.

"I guess. I just kept on growing til I bumped into something that felt like it might be nice knowing."

Cami was her name.

Jymee didn't really quite know what so attracted him to this cute little green growing thing. He was a tree, and she was quite different than he. But in a funny kind of way, it was nice to have her company to pass the day, share some different feelings of life, and her soft fuzzy roots were kind of nice.

Cami grew very fast, and within a few weeks was half the height of Jymee. He found that a little disturbing, but then again, she only had a few leaves.

"You're so much bigger than I ever dreamed," Cami told Seamore, as she gazed in wonderment down his meandering clear-blue stream "How far to do you go?"

~sea

~I dweem

"The sea? You dream? And how far away is the sea?"

~away ~away

"Well maybe someday."

~wain
~lots of wain
~and sno

"No, please don't say snow, or I'll have to go down below."

"Below?" Jymee asked.

"I can't take the cold," Cami confessed.

nibble nibble nibble

"Oh!" Cami gasped as she glanced Jymee's way. "There's something nibbling at your leaves!"

"My leaves? Jymee asked.

"Yes," Cami declared.

Where?" Jymee feared.

"On one of your uppers."

"Uppers? What is it?"

"I don't know," Cami said as she peered at the critter. "It's kind of long and fuzzy..."

"Fuzzy?"

...with lots of feet," Cami discovered.

"Feet?" nibble

"Yes, and it wiggles," she saw very clearly.

"Wiggles...?" Jymee nervously sputtered.

"Like wush, underneath."

"Wush? What's he doing up here? Cami, this isn't funny."

"We'll just have to watch and see how much he eats," Cami tried to comfort Jymee.

"But that could be all of me! Hey! What are you doing?" Jymee inquired of this wiggly wushing thing.

"Eating," answered the little critter after a few nibbles.

nibble nibble nibble

"Ya, but what you're eating is me!"

"Everybody's got to eat somebody," came in a casual burp of a reply.

"Who's eating you?"

"I don't know," the furry critter nibbled back.

"Great," Jymee sighed in frustration. "Well, do you plan on staying here long?"

"I don't know."

nibble nibble

"You don't know...?"

"I'm not really sure what I am," the critter matter-of-factly replied in a crunch.

"He doesn't know what he is," Jymee whispered to Cami in quiet distress.

"Somehow I thought I was gonna fly," the little nibbler replied.

"Fly?" Jymee asked.

"Butter.." was heard from the fuzzy wushy wiggling thing in-between bites.

"Butter? Fly? Could you be a caterpillar?" Jymee thought out loud.

"Yep...Caterpillar..." nibble nibble nibble

"Caterpillar? You're going to eat me alive!?"

nibble.....Gulp ~

"But where's he going to go?" Cami hesitantly inquired.

"I don't know. There's got to be other things to eat besides me," Jymee clearly insisted.

"How'd he get here?" Cami asked.

"I think I grew here," the caterpillar volunteered.

"Grew here? There's no way," Jymee declared. "I've been the only one growing in this place."

"I think I'm a present."

nibble nibble nibble

"A present.... A PRESENT?!!?!?," Jymee questioned quite horrified. "What kind of a present?"

"I don't know," the caterpillar timidly confessed.

"Jymee, let him stay," Cami encouraged. "He's really kind of cute. And I think he likes you."

"He likes me... Of course he likes me," Jymee replied. "He's hanging in my tree and eating all my leaves?!"

"It's only a few," Cami assured him.

"But that's all I've got?!..."

"You'll grow more," Cami said.

"But I just got these!?"

"That's part of being a tree," Cami tried to calm him. "The bigger you get, the bigger your family."

"This caterpillar is NOT my family!" Jymee insisted.

"Am I?" Cami asked.

"Well, yes... sort of. I mean I have feelings for you."

"I have feelings for you too, Jymee. And I think this little caterpillar needs you."

nibble

"Why me? I just became a tree, and now I've got a family."

"Jymee," Cami softly sighed, trying to find the words to make everything all right.

"Make sure he eats me evenly, okay?" Jymee surrendered. "I mean, I really would like to look half way decent while I'm growing through this thing."

"I'll watch him," Cami assured Jymee.

"Thanks."

nibble nibble nibble nibble nibble nibblenibble nibble

"Hey! Hey! Hey!" Jymee flapped at the munching critter who was suddenly making up for lost time.

nibble.....Gulp ~

"What's your name?" Jymee asked, as his tree stood silent.

"Twinkitoo."

"Slow down on that chew..."

nibble...

Three

Oh, to be a bee ~

April turned into May as Jymee finally reached the tippy-top of Tinystones for a view of the lake. It was a busy place. Seedlings popping out every which way.

Ducklings in troop fashion were waddling about the banks, scooting across water and leaving a mishmash of quacks and tracks in their wake. So too were the chicks scurrying about with partridge hens and the fawns with doe. And then there was Jo, a gnarly old lowhung Baldwin apple tree, buried in sweet smelling blossoms like wild-rose.

Offspring to a glacier, the lake was crystal clear and rich with springs, nestled in the foothills among oaks and maples, hickory and birch, spanning several miles in length by a mile wide—far too deep for anyone to ask how he came to be so wise.

On the lake's south side, at the edge of Jymee's view, was an island with its own forest of trees. It all seemed so familiar.

~ Maybe my acorn came from one of those trees ~
Jymee thought, not remembering his
snow-covered dream.

Twinkitoo had overeaten and turned into a cocoon. Jymee's leaves were well chewed, but more would grow back soon.

By now Cami was a few inches taller than he.

"Where are you growing so fast?" Jymee muddled as he stood in an after-rain puddle.

"Nowhere in particular," Cami pleasantly replied, "Why?"

"Well, could you wait for me? Every time I try to grow taller, I keep making more leaves."

Jymee noticed he was having more visitors, now that he'd turned into a tree. A hummingbird landed on him once, but didn't stay. Jymee was too wobbly.

The lake was a whole new world to him: sunshine and moonbeams dancing on rippling water between passing clouds and storms, and the rolling mist of the early morn.

One peaceful afternoon a week before June, Jymee felt a rumbling in Twinkitoo's cocoon.

"Are you in there Twinkitoo?" Jymee asked.

Wiggle

Wiggle Wiggle

~He sure wound himself up snug~ Jymee thought. "Now, how did you do that?"

Twinkitoo was the only one who could get himself out.

Jymee looked over at Cami and noticed a touch of pink at her peak.

"Cami, you have a little rash."

"Rash?"

"On your peak. I'll watch it," Jymee told her, "and make sure it doesn't turn into anything."

A few hours later, in a wiggle and a crack, emerged Twinkitoo from his sack, wet crumple-winged, exhausted, and stiff.

"What happened to you?" Jymee affectionately inquired.

"I can't talk. I'm too stiff," Twinkitoo replied, out of breath.

"That's okay," Jymee assured him. "We have all day."

Beneath the puffy pinks of sunset, Jymee felt a sudden knock at his trunk. It sounded like a flutter-bump.

flutter

bump

"Woooow...." was heard in a tiny nervous stutter from somewhere among the jiggling leaves.

flutter

bump

bump

flutter

"Cami. Look! Look who's flying?" proclaimed Jymee as a whisper of yellow fluttered out from his tree.

flitter

flutter

"Is that you Twinkitoo?" Cami marvelled, watching the yellow flutter come to a half-hearted stop on her peak.

flutter

flop

"Phew..." Twinkitoo murmured in a great sigh of relief, only to blow over and flutter-flop down to one of Cami's leaves.

"I'll never do that again!" Twinkitoo shuddered, clinging tight in the breeze.

"Never do what?" Cami asked.

"Be a cocoon."

"But look what you turned into!" Cami complimented the tiny flutter of yellow.

"Now what do I do?"

"Fly, Twinkitoo!"

Twinkitoo was a forest butterfly of yellow and grey, very aware of the shadows. They hid him by day.

He learned, early in his travels, to beware of the birds and the frogs and the spiders, but especially the dragonflies. They could scoff him up in mid-flight.

"Like lightning," Twinkitoo was told by other flightly friends of the woods. "Stay away from the lake. That's where they're born. A great dragonfly lives deep down underneath."

"You're on your own Twinkitoo," Jymee regretfully had to say. "I can't fly."

"Why?"

"I don't know," Jymee wondered himself, "but I keep trying."

Twinkitoo was up and off again, off into the shadows across the brook.

"Where are you going?" Jymee asked.

"I don't know."

Plickity Plunk

"Don't forget where you live," Jymee reminded Twinkitoo as he watched him disappear in a flittering flash of yellow through the trees.

~I wish I could get these leaves to catch a good breeze~ Jymee muttered in frustration to himself. ~But then what would I do with the the rest of me?~

The next morning, Jymee noticed Cami's peak was half pink.

"Cami, I think there's something very wrong.."

"Wrong?" Cami replied.

"Well,... your whole peak, it looks like.."

"It's going to flower, Jymee."

"But it's... Are you sure?" Jymee questioned quite perplexed.

"I can't really explain why, but I feel giggly deep down inside. Aren't you glad?"

"I guess I'm glad," Jymee replied, trying to be polite, not really sure about flowers and the like.

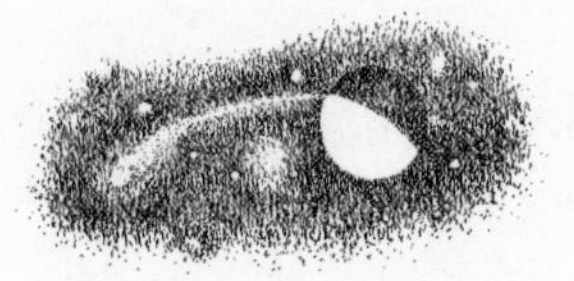

That night, as their leaves gently swayed in the balmy breeze to the lake's lazy waves lapping against the pebbly beach, one star... then two, shot across the sky.

"Did you see that?!" Jymee exclaimed.

"Oh,Yes," Cami replied, as they both stared into the sparkly night.

"They just zoomed across the sky, so free," Jymee envied "Not stuck like you and me."

"Do you feel stuck?" Cami asked.

"Well... Look at me. I'm a tree."

"I don't really feel stuck," Cami had to admit, in a gentle nudge from the breeze.

"You don't?" Jymee asked.

"No."

"But don't you wish you could fly?" Jymee wondered.

"Sometimes..." Cami replied. "It is kind of nice, though, to sit and watch everything else go by. You can get to know a particular place, see the changes around the lake. Seamore told me about a butterfly once. She was so busy laying eggs. She never had time to stop and think about things. To me, that isn't free."

"But to move my limbs," Jymee yearned. "Maybe go over there and take a swim like the ducks or fly like the geese. That's free. Now, the only way I move, is if something else is moving me."

"Maybe you're just learning to be a tree," Cami tenderly replied, as Jymee's lower branch came to glow from the perch of a lone little firefly who'd been out flickering way past his bedtime.

"Maybe you're right," Jymee reflected. "Sometimes, you make me feel like I have meaning under all these leaves."

Before the sun had a chance to wake, Cami's dainty pink slipper bashfully showed her face. It was like a soft inviting sunset, as the woods and the lakeside whispered her perfume, in leftover starlight dancing on the morning dew.

"My... my...," Jymee sighed, still mostly asleep. "I had the most incre...dible dream. There was you... and me...," he casually recalled, "and this... this... this... "

The morning smelled so sweet. Jymee couldn't quite remember his dream, but it sure felt nice being lazily buried in all his green. That was, until he suddenly realized his green was keeping company with all this pink.

"Oh!? Oh my..., "Jymee gasped as he quietly peered above his leaves. "Where did you come from?" he whispered. All he could see was Cami's pink.

Well I," Cami tried to reply. "I..."

"You are the prettiest flower I've ever seen!"

Cami blushed.

"And you smell so good. Was all this inside you?" Jymee marvelled.

"I guess."

"Oh My..." bzz..

An hour didn't go by before sunrise, as a bumble bee came buzzing on through, checking out some prim-rose and forget-me-nots, until the breeze sent him in the direction of Cami's perfume.

...

"Hey. Shoo. Shoo!" Jymee tried to distract the bee.

"Cami? Shoo... Shoo."

bzzzzz...

"Yes?" Cami replied.

"Something just landed on your lip. Creepy crawly.... Yuk."

"It's a bee," Cami giggled.

"You! Shoo! Shoo!"

Jymee could hardly contain himself, as the bee disappeared down inside her flower.

"Hey! You buzz on out of there, you buzzing thing!" Jymee insisted.

"Jymee. He's a friend," Cami tried to explain.

"A friend? Then how come I haven't met him?"

"You don't understand. I'm a flower."

"Ya, so..."

"Well... someday you'll have acorns, and they'll drop, and somebody'll come and carry them off. If the acorns are lucky, they'll get buried and grow into trees, and that'll be your gift for having bore the seeds."

"Okay... So, is he still down there?"

"Yes." bzzzzz...

"What's he doing?" Jymee asked.

"Just getting my seeds all over his feet."

"Great...," Jymee replied, feeling frustrated and rejected.

"Jymee. I'm a flower. And the only way my seeds get anywhere is with the wind and the bees, or anything else that happens to brush me.

"But I wouldn't mind doing that myself."

"You're welcome to, but you can't. You're a tree."

"I'll never understand why I decided to be one of these."

"You might not have met me," Cami lovingly replied, as the bee took off with a fur full of pollen.

"That's true," Jymee agreed, after awhile. "It would be nice if we could be the same thing."

"You mean, like two trees?" Cami asked.

"You could maybe be a cute little green fuzzy one," Jymee replied. "Like the one over there."

"But why?"

"Then I could understand you."

"Don't you feel like you do?"

"In a way, but I'd like to be closer."

"You can't get any closer than my roots."

A few hours later Twinkitoo came sauntering in from a morning of adventuring and immediately homed in on Cami's perfume.

flutter

flitter

flop

"Oooooo", Twinkitoo echoed as he ventured down inside her flower.

"This is n-eeeeeeeet... lucky, lucky me ~ ~ ~ ~ ~ ~"

"Twinkitoo! Would you get out of there, please?" Jymee meddled.

"Ooooooooooooo" Twinkitoo giggled, immersed in pleasure.

"Jymee, let him be. He's just exploring me."

"That's what I was afraid of..."

Jymee got used to Cami's collection of admirers after awhile, especially when he started to take note of all the critters crawling on his own leaves and bark.

"Doesn't anybody have any privacy anymore?"

Climbing is half the fun of having a tree in your own backyard.

As spring bowed her head to the rise of summer's blue bells and lilies, Cami, too, felt herself beginning to fade with the forget-me-nots and windflowers.

"Cami, stand up," Jymee nudged in a tickle.

"I am standing."

"You aren't."

"But I am," Cami insisted.

"Well, then how come you're bent?"

Jymee just knew something was wrong. She looked a little peak-ed and pale.

"Are you feeling okay?" he asked.

"I'm feeling fine." Cami replied.

Jymee spent the afternoon with her roots snuggly tucked and intertwined.

"I don't know why you cling to me so," Jymee jested. "I must just be one those irresistible kind of trees. But I'll get used to it."

"Oh, Jymee," Cami lovingly mused at his tease.

As the sun dipped in a kiss behind the hills, Cami's peak came to rest in the mossy softness of the water's edge.

Beneath the stars, Jymee affectionately looked at her frail tiny frame.

"What am I gonna do with you?" he said.

"Keep me I guess," Cami replied in a giggle upside

down. "But it is kind of funny to be half dangling down like this."

"See that clump of stars up there with the tail? " Jymee said gazing up at the big dipper. "They do it all the time. Sometime in the night they must turn upright or downright, but tomorrow they'll do it again. You'll see. Now, just rest on me."

~ Oh please dear moon ~ Jymee quietly pleaded from the tippy top of his tree, ~ send the sun soon ~

As the dew on Cami's droopy leaves was nudged to wake by a sparkle or two from the first peek of day, she knew in her heart she wouldn't be able to stay. Her journey was done.

"I have to go, Jymee."

"Go where?"

"The otherside of spring. Where I came from."

"Why?" Jymee asked.

"It's a part of my life. I loose my stem."

"But what about me?"

"You loose your leaves."

"Does that mean I'll never see you?"

"I'll be back...again, in the spring."

Jymee couldn't help but be sad. He felt like he was losing his better half.

"Don't be sad, Jymee," Cami softly said. "I'll just be underneath. We can still tickle and snuggle and before you know it, I'll green. But I will miss this warm sun and the breeze and the dew and seeing you."

"I'll miss you, too," Jymee said.

"All these purples and yellows and blues and pinks...," Cami said, as she looked around and collected memories to hold in her pillow for dreams.

"...The fireflies and the crickets and the birds and the moon. I do so want to remember you. And Twinkitoo's flutter." Cami put that in her pillow too.

"And your floppy green leaves," Cami told Jymee. "You were the very first touch of spring to me.

"I may have made a flower, but just being here... That was the biggest flower for me."

Jymee felt Cami slowly begin to sink to her roots.

"I've got you. I've got you," Jymee assured her, as he held her close.

"Watch over Seamore," Cami asked.

"I promise...I will."

"He'll be watching you too," Cami whispered last, in parting with her flower past.

Jymee sat in silence, wanting to cry, staring across the stream into the woods. But asking why? She was still there. She'd only left her flower behind. A sweetness that made its mark on his heart, like the afternoon sun when it cast her shadow on his bark.

~ I love you ~ Jymee sang to himself, ~ Seems so simple, but I love you... I do. ~

"I can still see you, dear Cami," Jymee sighed, "and smell you, and feel you. You left your shadowtracks on my heart."

Twinkitoo came fluttering in that night, by starlight, intending to sleep on Cami's leaf, only to find her laying nestled in a green mossy pillow by Seamore's stream.

"What happened?" Twinkitoo reluctantly asked, as he brushed her stem with his two tiny front feet, hoping to bring back her flower, again.

"She's resting awhile," Jymee gently replied.

Twinkitoo fluttered over and set down on one of Jymee's leaves. His touch reminded Jymee of another time, another summer, a dandelion and the stream.

"I wonder what it would be like to be a star?" Twinkitoo said as he stared into the night sky.

"It could get pretty lonely, I bet," Jymee said.

"Oh no, they sing," Twinkitoo insisted.

"They sing?" Jymee asked.

"I don't know how I know. I just know," Twinkitoo replied in a sleepy sigh, as he snuggled in on one of Jymee's leaves, while Jymee watched the mist settle in, and tuck the lake to sleep.

Four

Ripple ~

I got d'em apples
    D'em yeller-red ripe apples."

By August, Jo was overloaded and drooping with yellow red stripe'd fruit.

"I got d'em apples
D'em yeller-red ripe romp'n apples."

"What are you gonna do with all those things?" Jymee asked.

"D'ems my seeds   Spit'n image of me. You'll know when you start mak'n these."

"Those?"

"Apples, nuts...makes no mind. You still gotta tree down the line."

Since Cami went underground, Jymee spent most of his time just watching the lakeside. There was the dingy neighborhood loon, who didn't know if he was a bird or a fish, and some snoopy racoons, not to mention a few tanky turtles and that broadsided beaver....

"I remember you."

... and frogs, lots of frogs. Croak Croak

Croak

He had watched them grow from tadpoles.

~ They used to be fish ~ Jymee thought. ~ I don't get it ~

Lots of beginnings look nothing like their end.

~ But how could they breathe in all that stuff? ~

How can a tree fit in a nut?

A solitary salamander, missing an arm, slowly slithered on by.

slither

"What do you think,"Jymee asked the slithering little fellow.

"I don't," the salamander huffed.

slither

"What happened to your arm?" Jymee inquired.

"Got tored off."

slither

“Oh.”

“It’ll grow back.”

slither

“It will?”

“Just a limb,” he said in a slither, “I got me more important parts.”

slither

“You live under old Tinystones. Does he ever talk?” Jymee inquired.

slither

“Nope...”

slink

The salamander disappeared under the rock.

Twinkitoo
never returned
to Jymee’s tree.

“Must be out slaying dragonflies,” Jymee told his leaves, but deep down inside, he knew Twinkitoo had probably gone the way of Twink. Jymee had a dream one night: Twink and Twinkitoo were playing tag on a clover covered hillside.

Plickity Plunk

But Cami was fine. Every once in awhile Jymee would feel a fuzzy kind of smile deep down inside.

~I sure do like that cute little root~ Jymee told the moon.

Fall arrived and Jymee's leaves turned as red as wine.

"Why do they have to go, Jo?"

"Well, us trees, the ones with the leaves, we gotta shed our greens, let'm fall and cover our feet and lots a other things. That snow can get pretty cold, you know, and our roots are what keep us go'n."

"Brr...," Jymee shivered at the thought.

"That's a tree for ya, though," said Jo.

"But..."

"Look Jymee, I wouldna had any apples if there'd never been a freeze; and it took twenty-five years of freez'n to start grow'n these.

"And see how far my limbs reach? My roots got the same reach beneath. Same with your tree. That's a whole lot of territory if you ask me.

"So you go ahead and keep your leaves. A load a snow'll build up so, that one hefty wind'll whip through and break those branches a' yours right in two."

"Ow," Jymee trembled at the thought.

"Then all you'll be is a stub with a lot of roots."

"Yuk."

"Well, then let'm go," said Jo. "You'll grow new ones."

"I guess I just feel a little naked," Jymee replied.

"Modesty. Poof! We all look like this."

Jymee quietly said good bye to the leaves as they fell one by one.

With the last, he got a hard knotty feeling inside. They all sat around the base of his trunk.

~ I know other trees go through this, but they're not me. Maybe I wasn't meant to be one of these. ~

"Just don't look down," Jo said. "Look up. If you hadn't let go the first time, you'd still be a nut.

The last of the geese passing through from the North, forty in number, restlessly stood on the lake's shore. One call, some flaps, and some kwacks. They were up... and gone.

~ It doesn't make any sense ~ Jymee thought. ~ When everybody else is going off, I have to stay behind... and wait for them to come back over the mountain again. ~

Trees don't fly.

~ Well, I can still try... ~

Seamore kept on with his usual babbling.

~noflo~nogwo~

~noflo~nogwo ~

~ How come you never complain, ~ Jymee asked, as he stared into the basin at one side of Seamore's bank.

In the glassy reflection, Jymee saw a bare little tree having one tiny shiny just-uncurled green leaf eagerly flapping in the breeze.

"Little leaf," Jymee gently confided," I have to tell you this is no time to be turning green. I really think you ought to go back and be something else until after winter's through playing with your tree. It's not easy out here in this cold. I know. I'd have leaves too if I could, but..."

A giant old maple leaf, scarlet and aged by the trunk of a grandfather tree, interrupted Jymee's conversation as it casually floated down into view, creating ripples in its gentle swirl about the basin's pool.

ripple ~

"Hello? Hello?" Jymee called through the ripples as he lost sight of the little green leaf.

ripple~

"I was talking to a leaf," Jymee told the intruder. "Now, where'd it go?"

ripple~

Two little ants were riding atop the scarlet grandfather float, in search of a direction they didn't know.

"Off here... Off here. "

"Where? Here?"

"No.Here.."

"Not HERE??!.. "

Drifting to sit for a spell by some fern that stretched out over the stream, the two little passengers were temporarily free to take leave.

"Here! Here!"

"Hey! Hey!"

As the weeks passed, Jymee kept seeing that one little green leaf, wondering deep down inside if that tree really lived in the stream.

Til one day the leaf was gone. Jymee sat back reflecting in the sun, mimicking Seamore's murmur, and trying to make some sense of it all.

~noflo~nogwo~

~noflo~nogwo~

"No flo... No gwo...No flow... No grow... Are you talking to me? " Jymee asked Seamore.

noflo~ nogwo~
Loo kat me~ I um fwee~
Onli west~ my basin sees~

pond gwos old~
nowain~ nosno~
cownt~ yow~ bles~ sings~
let~ em go~

noflo~nogwo~
noflo~nogwo~

One sunny crisp afternoon, a man came walking through the quiet snow covered woods. He took out an axe and started chopping the green furry tree, the one on the forest side of the wall near Jymee.

chop
chop
chop

She fell in a bounce of fuzziness to the ground.

The man hung the axe back on his belt, and reaching down, took hold of her trunk, dragging her off in the snow...

swish~~
swish~~

...back from where he came.

swish~~
swish~~

All that was left in the small clearing was a stump and a trail.

There wasn't a sound around, just this empty hollow feeling like a part of home was gone.

A blistery storm cut through the lakeside that night.

Jymee did all he could to stay warm.

"Brrrr... Can't you blow somewhere else?" Jymee pleaded with the wind. "I'm so cold..."

Jymee held Cami tight.

"We're gonna be fine, dear Cami. Just hang on to my roots for awhile."

The snow didn't stop, though, for another night. And when the sun finally did peek through, it was only by luck that Jymee, in a coat of ice, still had a view. He was too numb to feel his roots.

"Are you okay down there?" Jymee jiggled. "Stay close. I'll get you warm."

But as day turned to dusk, Jymee noticed Cami's fuzzy feelings were gone.

"Cami, I know you're there. Please just move or squeak."

There was nothing—just Seamore's murmur and a few stars in the night, twinkling.

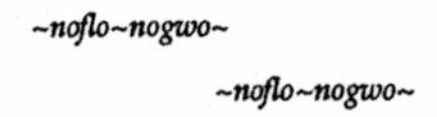

~I'm all right dear Jymee~ echoed softly that night through Jymee's dreams. ~It was only time for me to leave. See me in my flowers and the butterflies and the bees, if you need to see...but I haven't left your heart. There I'll always be, long after you've forgotten me~

~Cami...~ Jymee called out still half asleep, feeling lonely and confused, like only half a tree.

He stared at the lake peacefully glistening beneath the silhouetted hills.

* jingle *

jingle *

A white whisper of a glow, trailing in all the colors of the rainbow, sailed across the starlit sky, as Jymee heard in the twinkle of a hush...

~She's only resting awhile~

jingle *

Jymee started to cry.

"But she's not here."

He made icicles in his tears.

~I am, dear Jymee~ echoed Cami, as Jymee sunk down to her roots and hung onto every word.

~I'm in a quiet space, now...so much bigger than you ever saw me to be. Don't look down. Look around. I'm in everything~

As the stars began to share the twilight of another dawn, Jymee gradually drifted off to sleep, holding tight a pillow he'd made of Cami's rememberings.

Jymee spent the rest of the days til spring, hibernating. Over and over in his mind, he played back the words he'd heard that night.

The spring thaw melted so, that Seamore swelled and overflowed. Jymee was drenched to the end of his tap.

"Enough is enough is enough," Jymee pleaded. "She said she'd be back."

Jymee just had to wait for Seamore to feel better too.

Meanwhile, there were some new neighbors on the otherside of the bank: two little crocus.
"Aren't you out a little early?" Jymee asked.

Spring

Spring

"Oh no, we're trumpets!" they declared.

Jymee was pretty tall by now. He had to be at least three feet. We're not talking little ground shrub anymore. We're talk'n tree!

~ The birds even notice me. ~

Soon after his leaves began to uncurl, he developed these tingly stems of tiny yellow flowers.

"What am I doing to myself?"

Then came some more, popping out next to the others. The flowers attracted the birds and the butterflies and the bees...

Happy Birthday
Happy Birthday

...everyone in the forest it seemed, as Willie, a lakeside duck was remembering:

"We were waddl'n down the millrace,
all my fluffy friends and me,
when Elmer a yeller stripe'd bumblebee
ambled on by, a whispering
Jymee, he's got flowers!'
'Oh me...Oh my...' was heard among all the feathers
flying. 'We gotta go on by and at least say 'hi."
So with a wreath of lilac boughs,
we primped and waddled on down.
"Happy Birthday Happy Birthday.
Look at 'em.
Darn it if they aren't yeller ones!'"

Before Jymee knew it, he was developing these nuts.

The acorns attracted the squirrels...

"You-woo-woo-guys tickle."

...and more birds.

He had to admit, he was starting to feel
quite fatherly.

A furry grey squirrel, determined to take this
particularly large acorn off Jymee's limb,
twisted and tugged...

"Ouch!

...and twisted and tugged, jiggling the tree enough to
make Jymee dizzy.

"Stubborn thing," the squirrel remarked in disgust.

"It'll let go, when it's ready to let go," Jymee assured
the squirrel in his struggle to break free the nut.
"When'll that be?" the squirrel impatiently puffed.

"I don't know," Jymee replied.

So the squirrel came back another time, and...

Pop!

... the acorn dropped...

plickity plunk... plunk

....sending Jymee swaying for some time with the
rest of his nuts.

By summer's end, Jymee was beat. He looked over, as Jo gave a great sigh of relief, having dropped a full load of would-be baby trees living inside the seeds of each one of those yellow-red stripe'd things.

~Now I know why you slump,~ Jymee thought.

Jymee watched his leaves and nuts take off on their own wayward journeys to spots he knew not, rolling and tumbling and swirling. And then there were those who just plain preferred to stay where they'd dropped.

As winter settled in, Jymee sat back and reflected on the change, wondering where Cami might be. He gazed out through the trees standing in all their winter simplicity, framing patches of night where his favorite clump of stars stood low in the north sky.

"Snowflakes fall," Jymee sang to himself, "and I wonder where you are... Winter's breeze echoes through the trees..."

*

~It's Christmas Eve.
~It's Christmas Eve

...the stars seemed to sing.

*

Plickity Plunk

That night, as the snow-dotted lakeside slept in the crisp clear mountain air, the moon told a story for those who were quiet enough to hear:

Once there was a snowflake
whose journey it thought was to be
one of drifting south, growing fluffy,
and falling in love with a particular leaf.

The dream of someday meeting him
as he moseyed on down stream,
helped to pass the time when she was stuck in drifts
of snow or wedged against sleepy branches
and other colossal things.

Nestled one afternoon at the root of an old oak tree,
sadly sat our little snowflake friend
about to burst into a weep.

Her journey had been so long, it seemed,
much too long to ever bring her to the stream.

But in a whisper from the root it was heard:
"It's not the leaf you seek.
It's me, the tree.

I'm the love that begot your dream.
And you're the love that will bring the spring."

It was with that, a leaf fell from the tree,
the leaf she'd seen so often in her dreams.

In a gentle curl to enfold her,
snowflake warmed to a tear.

"It's not the end," said the leaf, "It's the blend.
That's why we're here."

Plickity Plunk

—ShadowTracks—

Wyntree

PART II

Five

Giggle ~

As any brook would if he could, Seamore ambled his way down through the spring-waking woods dressed in tiny green beginnings and speckled with dutchman's breeches, sweet white violets, starflowers, and crickleroot.

Winter had left behind a present of puddles and a christmas wreath of streamlets who'd eventually find their way home to Seamore's banks, but for now they were playing hide and seek about the twigs and leaves and giving rides to all sorts of nuts and seeds.

Down by the old hickory tree, the brook made a fork to the north, and didn't meander far, before finding himself abruptly interrupted by the ambitions of a plump furry beaver who'd sculpted a pond of his banks, nestled at the bottom edge of a sunny open meadow that looked out over a dell at some rolling woods.

Oh what a wonderful pond, thought all who lived in the woodside, a great place for bird baths, and lily pads and turtles and such. How could Seamore be upset? It was a puddle present. The best!

Dusty pink clover and buttons of yellow buttercups covered the meadow's top, bouncing off puffs of wind that tickled petals in their flops.

It was so much fun being a flower, the flowers thought, home to the bumble bees and the butterflies, and a nibble or two for some moles and mice, not to mention all the other nibblers in sight.

Not far from the pond's edge, hidden among all its yellows and pinks, lived a tiny blue-green beginning named Wyntree.

"How long does it take to flower?" Wyntree asked a buttercup nearby.

"When you start feeling pretty inside," said the buttercup. "It'll make you want to giggle. You won't really know why."

giggle

giggle

giggle

Wyntree heard a trickle of gigglers nearby.

"See," the buttercup politely perked up. "Those giggles are going to be flowers in awhile.

Wyntree looked around at her blue-greenness. It was just blue-green, not a hint of anything else.

"It takes time," some clover reassured her. "And besides, you do look a little different than us."

"Different?" asked Wyntree.

"Well, she's not clover or buttercup," the flowers agreed.

"Oh, dear me" Wyntree feared.

"It's not important," said the buttercup. "You're still going to flower. You'll see. Some of us grow to be pink or blue or yellow or white. Some are tall or small. We're all different sizes. Nobody really knows when they're going to flower. But when we do, we just flower and flower til the wind blows us free with all our petals and seeds."

giggle

giggle

"It's all part of being green," the clover agreed.. "And with the wind, we never know where we're going to grow. We only know we're going to flower."

Being around the buttercups and clover sure was nice. Whatever Wyntree was going to be, at least she knew she was going to flower. They told her to enjoy being green and little. She could watch the butterflies and the ladybugs and the bees, humming and fluttering about the yellows and pinks. There'd be plenty of time for the flowerside of things.

One bright dewy morning, Wyntree woke to find the world around her had changed. There were no more yellows and pinks that she could see in all the six inches tall she'd come to be.

~They left so quietly~ Wyntree thought. ~I didn't even hear them say good bye. There's got to be at least one clump of clover left.~

Not one clump had stayed behind.

Down the way, Wyntree noticed a green and blue-violet top spiked to the sky.

"Where did all the pink go?" Wyntree asked the blue-violet flower.

"The pink?" he replied. " Only us asters and blue-bells live here now with some queen anne's lace and sundrops. Why? Is pink your flower?"

"I'm not sure," Wyntree told him. "I think I have to wait awhile."

Wyntree watched the summer daisies bring in the dandelions and black-eyed susans and goldenrod. In a whisper, flowers would say goodbye amidst the trickle of giggles that brought other flowers to life. The meadow seemed to be just as happy in its new colors of blue and yellow and orange and violet and white.

Every sun-sparkled day would close its eyes just in time to greet the early evening's flickering fireflies making their way about the hillside, as the night brought out all its twinkling lights.

~ All these twinkles ~ Wyntree wondered. ~ What is the twinkle in all these lights?"

One evening she asked a passing firefly.

"Why do you flicker?" Wyntree asked.

"Flicker?" the fly replied.

"Like the sun does all day and sparkles do at night," Wyntree explained.

"You don't ask a flicker why it flickers, or it won't flicker," he curtly replied in a flicker, as he flicked out of sight.

The next afternoon as all the flowers were feeling a tad wilted and weak, grey and white clouds drifted by in the sky and surprised the meadow with raindrops. It felt so good to feel their plops. It had been quite some time since their last stop. All the flowers sprinkled each other in jiggles to make the moment last.

Wyntree looked out across the valley and saw another bunch of clouds about to make a stop. Their puffy pillows turned into billows that swelled to a pop and, in a mist, oodles and oodles of raindrops trickled out.

"I bet that meadow is as happy as us," Wyntree declared to the flowers as she suddenly saw all these colors in the sky, snuggled together, stretched from meadow to meadow.

PINK ORANGE YELLOW BLUE GREEN

"Petals!" Wyntree shouted. "Look! That's where the petals went! They're coming back to say hi."

Wyntree

Six

Honk~

Summer edged its way to Autumn, as the sun sank to sleep behind the mountains a little earlier each night. There didn't seem to be as many flowers or flutterings. Maybe the meadow was just taking a nap, Wyntree thought.

Down by the pond lived some wild mint and violet and pickerelweed the deer loved to eat—and frogs and worms, lots of worms. But even so, the pond wasn't having its usual company.

Lingering amidst the meadow's brown and brittle rememberings of a summer filled with giggles and joy, stood Wyntree feeling sort of empty and lonely as if all the flowers had gone and left behind their broken and used up toys.

"Nobody lives here anymore," Wyntree told a tiny bright white powder puff cloud taking a solo sail across the September-blue sky. "Sure there are racoons and rabbits and moles and mice, but where did all the colors go?"

Wyntree looked down and around at all her blue-greenness. "I'm the only color I know," feeling dressed up with no place to go.

A crow squawked and squawked again as he flew over the pond and down towards the dell. A dell Wyntree suddenly discovered was filled with all kinds of greenness, a green she'd forgotten was there.

"Silly me, " Wyntree remarked as she beamed to see green along the sides of the meadow and green rolling from hill to hill.

"Look at all that green! And here I was too busy looking at all the brown on the side of this hill."

As the days passed through October, Wyntree noticed the greens of the trees turn to yellows and oranges and reds.

"It must be their time to flower," Wyntree guessed.

The pond had its whirlwind of colorful visitors too. Feathery flapping flocks of honking geese who would circle and land for a splash every afternoon.

They said they were riding south on the wings of the sun's warmth, but they'd be back again in the spring when the sun turned north.

The days grew shorter and then one chilly eve the frost settled in. Wyntree had been told by some moles to watch for winter after the ground grew stiff.

The pond stopped having its honky visitors and the hillside's colors gradually fell away. Only brown and grey spindly silhouettes remained.

There wasn't anything looking like Wyntree that she could see, staying green amidst the tumbling leaves that danced across the frost in the crisp air that beckoned winter. Even the sounds had changed. No more ikits or flickers or croaks.

The chickadees and robins and bluebirds still flew in and out of the woods, and sometimes a rabbit or deer would leave behind a few tracks in the frost as they made their meadow cross.

"But no one lives in the meadow anymore," Wyntree sadly said to herself.

The wind took on a cold biting air, so cold it made Wyntree feel like she wasn't welcomed there, anymore. One morning she woke to find herself all twisted and bent.

"I thought you were my friend," she said to the wind.

Snow came and buried Wyntree in a drift made by being in the way of a meadow that was accustomed to a smooth and flawless face. It was so very hard to understand why she, in all her greenness, was still growing in this place.

Inkling by inkling, Wyntree felt the snow melt away, as the sun's warmth caressed the meadow in his crossing over that day. It was the first time Wyntree could remember feeling really loved, at least since the flowers went away.

But the quiet cold of dusk told Wyntree the sun couldn't stay.

"I wish you wouldn't be gone so long," Wyntree told the sun. "You're all I've got."

She watched her big bright red and yellow friend say good night, as she stood looking out over the cloud-covered icy browns and greys left behind. There wasn't even a hint of sparkle in the sky.

"Why? Why did I have to be so different than the rest? Why didn't I flower?" Wyntree sighed in the silence of her lonely and forgotten place.

The moon made its rise, as the clouds stepped aside enough for the sleeping snow to flicker here and there in the wake of the moon's sail across the night.

~Thank you~

Wyntree thought she heard an echo in all that quiet, but it must have been the wind she decided. Until another echo whispered by.

~ For being green~

"Green?" Wyntree asked.

~For being green ~

~Thank you.~

The echo seemed to come from the meadow's north side.

"Are you talking to me?" Wyntree hesitantly asked the wind.

"You're the only green," said the tall slender white curly-barked birch Wyntree saw standing tucked among the browns and greys.

"Yes. I guess I am," Wyntree replied, wanting to hide.

"The green of winter's spring" the birch said in a smile.

"Winter's spring?" Wyntree asked.

"You are the otherside of winter to us. A present. Thank you , little green," the birch whispered in the moon's reflection.

"You're welcome," Wyntree shyly replied, as she bundled up his words and snuggled down in her roots, feeling a little giggly inside after hearing from the woods.

~ A present, he said I was a present ~ Wyntree thought as she drifted off to sleep.

~ You are the meadow patch's Christmas tree ~ Wyntree heard in her dreams, as she saw a patch of lightness seemingly made of snowflake crystals and sunshine and mist, soft and gentle in its movement, cup and cradle her as if she were something found that had been dearly missed.

~Christmas tree?~ Wyntree timidly asked. ~But I don't know how to be.~

~It's all inside your tree,~ the light cheerfully assured her. ~We just have to bring it some spring~.

* twinkle * tingle *

From a hiding place deep down inside Wyntree's heart, appeared a tiny wooden box wrapped in oak leaves with an acorn top.

~In here~ the light tenderly said ~is all you treasure.~

From it, rose a sparkle of sunset that came and hung off her bough, while a grey and yellow butterfly popped out and flew about.

~The blue-green in your needles is the love the meadow holds for the stream, and every time there's a touch of water to your sprigs, the stream is saying 'I love you dear meadow green of my being. Wait til you see the flowers I bring you in spring.'~

From the box came another treasure in sprinkles of morning dew, as a dove came and perched for a song while the sun peeked through.

~ If you love this, love the snowflakes too ~ flickered the light, ~ for they're the winter's morning dew. They touch and tickle, and in the sun's love, make icicles, until the spring brings the puddles and pinks and greens and yellows. ~

Blue sky and a wisp of wind nudged Wyntree's peak, while a powder puff cloud snuggled in for a sleep. Trailing down and around appeared some pine cones, as one dropped from her tree into a stream weaving through the mountains sitting at her feet.

When she looked again at the box, there appeared a plump smiling moon.

~ When you smile ~ the light said, ~ the moon smiles too ~

It dangled off her lower bough, where beneath a clump of orchids came to flower and some geese flew south.

In looking again at the box, Wyntree noticed a flickering inside.

~ A star wants to come out ~ Wyntree was told by the loving wisp of sun-sparkled light.

~ A star? ~ Wyntree asked.

~ But it's afraid to shine. ~

~ Why? ~

~ The universe seems so big to that tiny light. But someday, she'll say 'Wait a minute! I have a right to shine!' And she'll come out of that box to see that home is really on the top of your tree ~

~ My tree? ~ Wyntree asked.

~ She's your little star. Take care of her, Wyntree. She's the sparkle in your heart. ~

~ Oh look how pretty you are ~ Wyntree heard as she was picked up with all her treasures and turned back down to bed.

~ When you were only the dream of a seed, I passed over this patch, thinking it so wished for a warm fuzzy Christmas tree. And then I felt the twinkle of your love for the stream. A candlelight in the meadow. That's what you are to me.

~ Where would winter be without your precious green. Sweet dreams, my little Wyntree ~ whispered the glow of Father Winter as a sparkle kissed her peak.

tingle *

* jingle *

In the lingering love of Wyntree's sleep, she felt a sudden jiggle to her tree.

"Please, not now," she mumbled, "I so want to sleep."

But the jiggle kept on jiggling.

"Okay, okay," Wyntree said as she felt forced to wake and see, the nudge of a reindeer's nose and a lick up the side of her tree.

Sunny morning tickles on Wyntree's icicles coaxed her to wake to a field dusted in fluffy white snowflakes. A few bluebirds were playing in the distance from tree to tree, as the pond sat beneath its icey hat, inviting feathered and furry visitors for a drink.

Wyntree looked around at all her blue greenness, thinking maybe she really might be a tree like all those spindly greys and browns, instead of a flower-to-be. But she was still green.

A bright red cardinal flew out of woods and stopped by the pond. He was as bright as a petal, Wyntree thought, riding on the wind. After a sip or two, he took off across the meadow and then circled back over by Wyntree's green.

"What a cute little tree," he chirped.

"Am I really a tree?" Wyntree asked.

"Why sure you are. You're a little green star," he said in a flap, as he turned to make his way south. "Can't you see? Your boughs even have sprigs sticking out."

Wyntree

Wyntree quietly examined all her parts. "You mean I'm not a flower?" she asked.

"Everything flowers," he assured her as he dipped out of sight.

Wyntree thought about the dream she'd had last night, and the birch tree on the hill. She could see him better now, standing as white as snow at the edge of the woods.

~ A Christmas tree. How can I be? ~
Wyntree quietly asked as she looked around the meadowpatch.

~Love being green ~

...came from the heart of curly-white bark.

Wyntree watched the snowflakes who had hugged her trunk in the early morn, melt into puddles with the sun's afternoon love, only to put on icey's hats again with the coming of dusk.

In the evening twilight, the stars felt like a halo about Wyntree's peak, as she stretched out her tiny boughs across the meadow just to see how far she could reach.

The moon was so full and bright that night. Wyntree thought it might be smiling too. There were icicle sparkles here and there in the woods with a trail of dancing sparkles winding down to the pond.

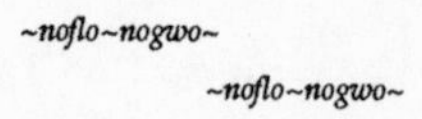

"Sometimes you're the only sound I hear," Wyntree said to the winding sparkles.

"Do you ever go to sleep? I heard your name is Seamore. Did a beaver really do that to your stream?

"I hope the puddle hasn't made too much of a muddle for you, but maybe you're used to those things.

"I was told you're always getting everyone's leftover nuts and twigs and leaves.

"Just think of them as presents. You really are very nice to have in the trees."

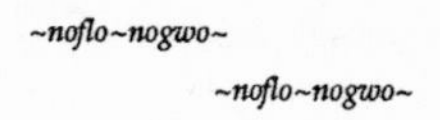

Seven

Ooh-who-who-who ~

Seamore's sparkles made their way upstream to the lake, where a gnarly old Baldwin apple tree lived named Jo. No one really knew how old he was, but his cranky twisted and knotty trunk told. He'd been around much longer than the oak who shaded the stream. The oak, whose name was Jymee, stood well into middle age it seemed. Jymee must have once sprouted right next to Tinystones, the stonewall, for now his trunk hugged and curled around the moss and ivy ladden rock as if the two had been married all along.

~ Dear friend..." Jymee reminisced to the breeze, as he gazed out across the afternoon snow. "It's been sometime since you've seen the sunshine through these trees. And the lake, with its contentment just to be a lake. Aah, but to be content to see life so lightly.

~ Yours and mine were of another time.

~ I never thanked you for all you've been to me. I stand rich and deep, passionate and loving because of you.

~It's been sometime since I've seen your smile, but you're always on my mind. The pictures I hold of you are many. And your dreams, I hold them too, for I know what they meant to you.

~That you're not with me, doesn't mean you're gone. When I think of you, you're there. Still that whisper of pink, who left her shadowtracks behind.~

"Jo," Jymee sighed as he drifted back from the shadows of his heart, "I must be getting old."

"I've noticed that too," Jo jested. "I was going to talk to you."

"No, really Jo. All these feelings, I lost so many years ago, have been coming back," Jymee confided. "The other night an old clump of roots felt so sad. It was as if it didn't want to live here anymore."

"The woes of winter," Jo replied.

"No. It was much deeper than that," Jymee remembered. "But I'm feeling better now. Whatever was lost must have been found. Funny thing, these roots. Sometimes they get all tangled up in knots. I'll be glad when spring comes around.

"Could have been indigestion," Jo offered as a thought.

"You know we don't get indigestion in the wintertime," Jymee replied.

"Well, maybe you were numb from the cold."

“I thought that too. You’re right,” Jymee confessed. “Maybe it is the cold. You’d think after all these years I’d adjust, but I don’t. I just about get thawed out and comfortable with leaves and then... “

“Come the bugs, the big creepy crawly bugs,” Jo bellowed.

“The bugs, you’re right,” Jymee agreed.

“Frankly, I’d rather have snow,” said Jo.

“But I do like all that green,” Jymee reflected as he stared at his barren bedfellows. “It gets so depressing to be around these browns and greys. Can you tell by the sun, how much longer we have to stand in this stuff?”

“Look at your buds,” Jo suggested “If they aren’t out yet, then there’s no sense looking up.

Wyntree felt she was almost always the first to greet the peek of day as she sat high on the mountain above the dell, and almost always the last to say good night to the sun as it dipped down behind the distant hills.

“Don’t be depressed,” she told the woodside. “Spring is coming. I can tell. If you don’t believe me, look at your buds. They’re just staying warm until after the chill. “

The winter winds tossed and tumbled snowflakes into puddles of spring, as Wyntree discovered one of her roots had managed to wiggle its way down to the pond and stick its toe tip in.

"Ouch!" Wyntree said as she felt something nibble her toe.

"Seamore, who's nibbling me?"

tad ~po wo wo~wo

"Tad-Po-wo?" Wyntree tried to understand.

"A tad-po-woole." Wyntree heard again in a clear low and slow sounding gurgle. "He thinks you're a bug."

"A bug?" Wyntree asked. Now she was really befuddled.

"A bug," Wyntree heard again, but Seamore didn't sound like his usual self. "Can...you... hear?" came to her very slow and very clear.

"Hear?" Wyntree repeated. It seemed to be coming from...

"Hear. Dow-oon he-re."

Wyntree felt an icey cold ripple where the tadpole had just bit.

"Here?" Wyntree wondered as she sunk deep down inside herself, to the tippy-tip of her root tip.

"Who's there?" Wyntree hesitantly whispered, sensing a friendliness of sorts on the outside.

"Seamore" came in a comfortable drawl back.

"Seamore?" Wyntree marvelled. "But you sound so clear."

"I should sound clear. You're inside me down here."

"Inside you?" Wyntree asked as she wiggled the tip of her root in an attempt to explore.

Ooh-who-who-who. Don't do that!" Seamore gurgled and poppled. "It tickles. A lot!"

Every part of Seamore seemed to speak in feelings of ebbs and flows. More feelings then Wyntree had ever known.

"I never knew there could be so many feelings," Wyntree told Seamore. "How do you keep them apart?"

"I don't," Seamore replied.

"Then how do you know it's me who's talking to you?" Wyntree asked.

"You twinkle...like a star," Seamore seemed to twinkle in a feeling back.

"Do stars have feelings, too?" Wyntree asked.

"Everything has feelings," Seamore rippled.

"I dreamt once that a star wanted to live on the top of my tree," Wyntree said "Does everything twinkle?"

"Twinkles are love," Seamore replied.

"But where do the twinkles go after they've twinkled?"

"They don't go," he assured her, "They ebb and flow, like day does to night."

Over time, Seamore taught Wyntree how to feel the way the water feels all the changes in the woods.

"I just felt a giggle up stream," Wyntree exclaimed. "Oh! And there's another one! Seamore, I think flowers are coming."

~flo wo~wo wos~ the woods could hear Seamore gurgle on down through the dell.

The morning arrived when the first of Seamore's stream garden came to flower, popping up in pantaloons of dutchman's breeches, and sweet white violets.

The meadow was showings hints of tiny green beginnings too, as clover and buttercups and a few forget-me-nots started to peek through.

Everyday the woods felt a little lighter and brighter, with each sleepy bud that uncurled to say 'boo.'

"Does this mean, when the trees green, I'll lose your sparkle view?" Wyntree reluctantly asked Seamore.

~noflo~nogwo~

"We all have to grow," Seamore gently reminded her.

Pinks and greens and yellows popped out about the meadow, while the spindly greys and browns of the woods began to grow green and plump and round.

"I wish you didn't have to go," Wyntree sadly told Seamore, as she watched his stream gradually disappear in a forest of spring.

~noflo~nogwo~

~I know. I remember. You taught me,~ Wyntree tried to assured herself. ~Twinkles don't go. Well, I still have your puddle present. And you still have my toe.~

The curly-white-barked birch could be seen standing among the other trees. A rabbit told Wyntree the birch was there for the woods to remember the otherside of spring.

There were tiny flowers and tall flowers, more flowers than Wyntree could have ever dreamed to see, rippling across the meadow and down to the pond where some lilies of the valley were basking.

That afternoon, Wyntree stretched in all directions to hug the spring's bouquet.

"Mmmmm, I'm so glad to see you," Wyntree said. "And I'm so glad I stayed."

Eight

Oh dear ~

There was a family of chickadees who came to live in Jymee's tree. Springs were always noisy, but he'd gotten used to those things.

One sunny morning while the birds were chirping away, some boys came in a boat and started dismantling Tinystones. One by one, his rocks were picked up and carried away.

The salamander who lived there then, was horrified.

"What are they doing? What are they doing?!" the salamander frantically paniced. "This is my home! Go away! Go away!"

Jymee offered a leaf, and as it fell to the ground...

"That won't do!" the salamander pattered. "I need some cold. Some dark. Oh dear... What'll I do? What'll I do?"

The salamander slithered over to the stream and hid under a rock.

By sundown, only a damp clay impression remained.

~noflo~nogwo~

~noflo~nogwo~

The salamander knew very well what Seamore was saying, but he still didn't like the change.

With Tinystones gone, Jymee had to admit, he felt a great weight had been lifted off his roots.

The only downfall might be Jo's apples.

"Now don't you guys get any ideas of roll'n over here," Jymee counseled the dangling fruit.

As the moon rose above the woods, Jymee remembered a warm inviting fuzzy wrapped-around spring-bouquet feeling that had come over him that afternoon.

"Jo, did you feel like you'd been hugged this afternoon?" Jymee asked.

"No. I was too busy watching Tinystones go."

"It was probably just the change," Jymee decided. "Maybe some rock got dropped on a soft spot."

Seamore's lily-ladened pond was the talk of all the dragonflies and frogs.

zing~ ~ ~ ~

zing~ ~ ~ ~

With the splashes and croaks and puddle plunks, it seemed almost as busy as when his honking friends had stopped by on their return from the south.

The clover had blown away with the breeze, but the buttercups said the bluebells and daisies would be popping up soon. A patch of teaberry found a way to grow snug up against Wyntree's trunk.

"I hope you don't mind," said the teaberry, "but anywhere else, doesn't feel like home to us."

Early that afternoon, a storm was in the brew. It was plain to see with all the flying petals and leaves.

"We're just cleaning house," Wyntree tried to assure anyone who would quiet down long enough to listen beneath the wind's howl, as it sent furry and feathered friends for cover under stumps and boughs.

wooO~

Howl

Lightning and thunder cracked and rumbled down through the sky, announcing the coming of some dark and grumpy clouds. Wyntree had never seen them quite this mad before now.

"You really shouldn't let your feelings build up like this," Wyntree told the clouds. "Maybe it would help if you rained more than once in awhile."

RUMBLE~

And with that, buckets and buckets of rain came tumbling down.

Wyntree stood in the pouring rain, as the wind whipped sideways across the hill, plucking soon-to-be petals before they'd even had a chance to know how a flower feels.

All Wyntree could remember was being alone, twisted and bent in that biting winter cold.

~At least if I were in the trees~ Wyntree thought, ~I wouldn't be having the wind tearing at all sides of me. But I have to be strong~ she declared huddling down in her roots away from the storm, ~because this meadow patch is where I belong.~

Wyntree remembered Seamore's sparkles, as she imagined reaching outside herself to give the mountain a hug. "It's going to be okay. Just think of all the presents we'll have when the sun comes out again."

Seamore's ripples had turned into roars, while tiny streamlets filled-up and gave Seamore all their toys.

ripple~ ~~

~~ ROAR~~

Down came nuts and twigs and leaves and petals galore, not to mention any passengers they might have had aboard.

"Off here... Off here. "

"Where? Here?"

"No.Here.."

"Not HÊRÊ???.. "

There was so much water, the puddle pond tipped and overflowed, sending lily pads and frogs for a ride down through the dell.

Croak~

What a spill!

RUMBLE~

ZAP!

"What was that?!" Wyntree gasped at the sound of a lightning zap that brought her to the peak of her tree.

"In the woods! Seamore! I feel it! Upstream!"

The thunder and lightning slowly moved on to another range of mountains as the sun sparkled through, making up for all the rain that had soaked the meadowpatch and the hills, too.

On the otherside of the forest, Jymee stood beneath a sky that had just stopped crying. His limb was split, one of his lowers.

"Now, what'd you go and do that for?" Jymee asked the sky.

"Are you okay?" Jo inquired.

"I'm not really sure," Jymee replied.

A bluebird flew over and sat on Jymee's broken bough, passing out some chirps as he dryed off his feathers and rubbed his beak on Jymee's bark.

"See," Jo jested, "He still thinks you're a tree."

"Thanks," Jymee replied, wondering why, when he was all broken and bent...why anyone would want to sit on him.

After a few chirps the bluebird fluffed and puffed, and then took off for the lake.

The woods didn't say very much for the rest of the day. It was time to be quiet and think about picking up the pieces and starting all over again. Nothing is ever really lost...just maybe not where you last thought..

The pond appeared a little squished and sat on, but it was still the best...even though a good many frogs and lily pads discovered they were living someplace else.

It seemed the stars must have been rained on too, for that night their sparkle was as bright as the moon.

"I guess this means goodbye," Jymee solemnly told his broken bough. "Thanks for hanging out with me all these years, while I was hanging out."

~ My nuts... My leaves... They're always taking off. That's okay. When it's time to go, it's time to go, I guess.

I wonder where that bolt of light came from anyway, ~

STAR ~~

Jymee thought he heard a crystal-clear something come from somewhere down in his roots.

"Star?" Jymee questioned.

FALLING ~~

~ Falling? Star?, ~ Jymee pieced together. "I did always want to meet one. But like this?"

"How would you know about stars?" Jymee suddenly discounted the hearsay. "You're down there, somewhere. Stars are up."

I'M FILLED WITH THAT STUFF ~~

If Jymee had been feeling a little better, he might have sunk down in his roots and checked out that nut.

~Besides, I've been told stars sing. And I didn't hear him sing,~ Jymee decided.

ting

tinkle

~Or Did I?~

Nine

Tender Spots ~

few mornings after the rain, a whimsical wooden-fluted melody echoed across the lake.

A kindly man came to visit. His name was Thoreau, the birds said. A friend to the lake, he'd often take morning dips and walks and write, and spend hours watching a bird's flight.

"Bet you're going to make some pretty tasty apples this year," Thoreau said to Jo as he passed by his heavy-ladened tree.

"And it looks like you could use a little help," Thoreau noticed, when he saw Jymee's broken branch dangling.

"I made this flute from a branch not quite as large as yours," Thoreau said, as he braced and wrapped Jymee with after-rain presents of leftover woodlands and vines...helping to bring his life back to upright.

"Yep, this flute has been a good friend. I thank that tree for the music it brings to me. "

"You'll be fine," Thoreau said as he patted Jymee on his trunk. "I'll come by again and check on you. Now get plenty of sun."

Jymee watched him walk away through the woods as a bright red cardinal followed. The two blended into the pinks and yellows and greens of a bashful rainbow that sat beyond the trees.

In the early part of evening, as the lakeside gave a sultry summer sigh, a light breeze came for a long-awaited visit to cool down the hot and muggy night. Jymee could feel it move in ebbs and flows across his leaves, gently drying the brow of his tree.

"It's nights like these, that a little bit of winter would feel so good," Jymee thought, as he took note of a curly-white-barked birch standing back in the woods.

~That little pine... ~ Jymee remembered as he looked down at the weathered and moss-covered stump of the one who used to live nearby. It was partially hugged by violets, now, and a clump of lady slippers about to take their summer bow.

"When you were green," Jymee said to the forgotten tree, "I wasn't very tall. In fact I could barely see over the wall. I remember the day a man came and took you away. But he didn't take your love. Your love stayed."

"That was a long time ago," Jymee said to Jo, "and it's been a long time since I've remembered that little tree ever lived by me."

"Maybe you ought to go down and see what's causing all the stir," Jo proposed. "Better to clear it up now, before you start growing mold."

Jo was probably right, Jymee thought. It had been sometime since he'd taken a long hard look at his roots. "I guess I've been too busy growing up all these years," he confessed.

As Jymee turned down below, it wasn't long before he bumped into a clump of musty old neglected feelings, all tied in a knot.

"What's the matter?" Jymee affectionately asked, as he touched the tender spot. "I didn't mean to cut you off."

It would just take a little time and understanding to un-knot the spot, Jymee thought.

In a moment of quiet reflection, a few words came tumbling out. "But she's not here," Jymee heard as he saw tiny icicles make tiny tears."

"But she is here," Jymee told the lonely little seedling-child who lived inside his tree, remembering so well the loss of his flower friend, Cami. "As long as we hold her in our heart, she's always here. That's what really matters. Don't be sad. Just remember her green and pretty and pink, playing with Twinkitoo."

With a little more tender silence, the knot timidly loosened to a snug. Inside Jymee could see a crumpled and over-loved pillow filled with memories wrapped around what was left of a tiny old root from a lady slipper flower.

"You can still hold on to that," Jymee said. "but maybe not quite so tight. We have to let go a little, so we can feel her love us back."

As Jymee sunk deeper, he passed through a bunch of ting-tinkling sounds. Some magical tourmaline crystals were growing off his roots in blues and greens and pinks and whites. Jymee couldn't see them, but that's what a groundhog had told him once.

tinkle ting
ting tinkle
ting

~ Star stuff ~ Jymee thought, remembering the ting-tinkles from the other night. ~ Must have been me, getting sentimental and sappy. How would you know anything about stars? Stars are up! ~

tinkle

Jymee sunk deeper and deeper, down into his newest part . It was so fresh and vibrant and filled with spring. Aah, to be young again, Jymee thought.

When he came to the tip of his root, he decided to probe around, and feel what was down and up.

"Aaaaaaa," came in a sudden scare, from out of nowhere.

"Aaaaa," Jymee yelled back. The scare was so scarey, he couldn't help but react.

tinkle

ting

ting

Who's there?" Jymee whispered, after the jiggling stopped.

"Me. And that tickled. A lot!" gurgled and poppled back. "Darn it! Everybody's always doing that!"

"Me? Who's me?" Jymee politely inquired.

"Seamore."

"Seamore? You don't sound like Seamore."

"That's because I'm not talking with a mouth full of twigs and leaves. You're inside me down here," Seamore informed him.

"Inside you?"

"You've got a root hanging out between two rocks in my stream."

"So that's where I'm at," Jymee laughed at learning where he sat.

There were all these feelings, more feeling than Jymee had ever experienced in one spot. "Are you the reason I was feeling so sad this winter?" Jymee asked, recalling that those winter feelings seemed to be so much deeper than those of that knot, way back.

"Oh my goodness, no," Seamore gurgled and poppled.

"But I'm pretty sure it came from this direction," Jymee said quite perplexed.

"Could be you just were listening to somebody else."

"Somebody else?" Jymee asked.

"I've got all kinds of fish and frogs and roots and rocks hanging out."

"That's a relief," Jymee decided as he turned back towards his top.

"Thanks," Jymee called back down from half way up. "I'll try not to tickle so much."

"Okay. I'll try not to yell," came gurgling back.

Jymee rose up from down below and stretched way out into the sultry evening breeze, dusting off the last of some cobwebs and musty old leaves.

"Mulch, they call it," Jo greeted Jymee's return. "All those years of leftovers. Be thankful. At least they're not petrified yet."

Jymee could always count on Jo to look on the brighter side of things.

"How'd it go down there?" Jo asked.

"Pretty well," Jymee replied. "I bumped into one tender spot. Got that loosened up, and the rest of the way was clear down to the rocks."

"Rocks?" Jo asked.

"You know, that groundhog was right. I do have crystals dangling off me," Jymee recollected from on top.

"Crystals?" Jo asked.

"They make ting-tinkles. That's all. Oh, and I bumped into Seamore."

"Seamore?"

"I have a root hanging out between two of his rocks. Seamore sounds so clear down there, Jo. You should have heard him."

"Must have been all those years with Tinystones," Jo concluded from the talk.

"Why would you say that?"

"Rocks. You sure do like rocks...alot."

Wyntree

Ten

In The Stars ~

It was one of those every-once-in-awhiles, when the day didn't want to say goodbye to the night, as the moon and an evening star stood patiently waiting their turn in the pastel shadows of the sky.

The day was in full bloom. It happens every June. Night will have her turn in winter. Father Sun knows it well. It's his favorite carousel.

"Might I ask, why are you hiding beneath that leaf?" Wyntree inquired of a bashful flower-to-be. "If you want to flower, you're going to have to stand tall enough for the sun to see."

"I'm afraid," trembled the tiny bud.

"Afraid? Of what?" Wyntree asked.

"Getting nibbled."

"Flowers aren't afraid of nibbles," Wyntree replied. "They just want to flower."

"Maybe I'm not a flower," the bud confessed.

"Everything flowers," Wyntree expressed.

"And then what?" asked the bud.

"On to the next flower, I guess."

"And where will that be?"

"Sometimes the same spot and sometimes not.
It doesn't really matter," Wyntree explained.
"Flowers are flowers. They don't worry about where they're at."

"See that star up in the sky," Wyntree said "That's a flower too. On the other side of day. It's a night flower. It just has different petals than you.

"Every star is a flower and every flower is a star. We all have twinkles. Twinkles are the love in our hearts.

"Oh my goodness, look at all those twinkles in the sky. Now tell me, why would you ever want to hide?"

"I guess I feel alone," the tiny bud replied.

"Hiding under that leaf, I can surely see why. You're not alone. You're part of this big wonderful meadow, and the meadow is our home.

"We couldn't be without the meadow or the sun or the wind or the rain. Sometimes it may get a little too windy or clouds may put on a grumpy face, but everything has it's season and reason. Besides, we make the prettiest flowers after it rains."

The day finally did say good night, as one by one, the stars took their place in the sky.

"Look. Even the stars live in meadows," Wyntree said to the bud, "and I bet not one of them is afraid of getting nibbled."

As Wyntree gazed at all the star-meadows in the sky, a shooting star sailed by.

~ I wonder, ~ Wyntree thought, ~ if that's the way a star-flower says good-bye. ~

In the peacefulness of twilight, Wyntree heard a soft seasoned sound come from somewhere deep down.

"Is the meadow my home?"

"Your home?" Wyntree asked. She could feel the sound all the way down to the tip of her toe in the pond. It could be an old grandfather fish or a turtle or a frog, she thought. Maybe even a waterbug. Seamore's got all kinds of things living inside the pond.

"My home... Is it my home, too?" came softly back.

"If you're part of Seamore, you're part of the meadow," Wyntree playfully replied.

"Well, only part of me is a part of Seamore," trickled back.

"And what part might that be?" Wyntree asked.

"A root. I have a root wrapped around two of his rocks."

"A root?" Wyntree asked. "It is the same with me."

"And what is your root a part of," the friendly voice inquired.

"A tree," Wyntree replied.

"A tree? That is me," came back in a laugh so inviting that even Wyntree couldn't help but laugh too.

"Tell me, what do you look like?" Wyntree shyly inquired. "Maybe I can see."

"Oak, middle aged," was his reply. "Not too far from a crotchety old apple tree."

"How did you find me?" Wyntree asked.

"I heard you," the voice replied. "speaking of meadows in the stars. Tell me who you are."

"I'm green and fuzzy, some say," Wyntree bashfully replied. "I'm not very tall. I don't lose my leaves or turn brown in winter. I stay green through it all."

"Are you a pine?" he asked.

"I think so. Are you far away?"

"I don't really know," he replied. "My name is Jymee and yours?"

"Wyntree," she told him as the pond began to stir. "I hope we meet again."

"Tomorrow?" Wyntree heard through the gurgles.

"Tomorrow," Wyntree agreed. "I'll wait by my toe."

Jymee stood out beneath the stars, staring up at the twinkling meadows stretched across the night. It was too dark to look for pines. But tomorrow. In the sunshine.

Jymee thought about his broken bough. ~Maybe it won't matter anyhow.~

"Wyntree..." Jymee whispered just to hear the sound. Listening to her down there seemed so different, as if she was inside him somehow.

Mor-ning sun-shine... Mor-ning sun-shine," Wyntree sang to the first touch of sun as it twinkled the dew dry.

"Can you feel that warm wonderful sun?" Wyntree asked the little bud still on-the-hide.

~There's an oak in my life~ Wyntree shyly considered, as she felt a wee bit giggly inside. ~An oak...named...

"Jymee..." she whispered, afraid an answer just might come tumbling back.

Wyntree bashfully explored Seamore's woodside down to the borders of the pond, and on down towards the dell.

~What if I see him?~ she thought. ~Maybe he'll think I'm too small.~

There was an oak and then another oak, lots of oaks, but not one seemed to be looking for anything fuzzy and green.

~I guess I'll just have to wait til he finds me~ Wyntree decided. ~Sometimes being different is easier to see.~

The afternoon brought a light breeze and a sunshower that perked up all the dusty greens. Everyone just wanted to be lazy and playful and not worry about anything.

"Jymee?"

Jymee heard a whisper from deep down inside. He knew that sound was Wyntree, as he curled down to say hi..

"Jymee?" he heard ever so faintly.

"Wyntree? Can you hear me?" he called back, as Wyntree delighted in seeing a twinkle.

"If I'm really quiet inside, I can hear you," Wyntree replied. "Oh I hope Seamore doesn't stir again soon.

I'd like to talk to you awhile. Did you feel the sunshower?"

"Rain danced on my leaves and ran down my bark. I love it when it rains," Jymee shared, as he caressed the thought.

"I looked for you today," Wyntree confessed.

"I looked for you too," Jymee was quick to reply, "but I forgot to ask how tall you are."

"I'm not very tall. In fact I'm very very small."

"That's okay," Jymee assured her.

"There are oaks around me," Wyntree told him, "but I couldn't tell if one was you."

"Did you see an old apple tree with red and yellow strip-ped dangling fruit?"

"No," Wyntree replied.

"I'm right by the stream," Jymee told her.

Wyntree looked around. There was not an apple tree to be seen.

"I live by the pond," Wyntree told him.

"The lake is the only pond I see," said Jymee.

"Maybe the lake is the pond," Wyntree hoped.

"Is there an island with trees?"

"There are some cat-tails and lily pads," Wyntree volunteered.

"This island is big."

Wyntree thought about it, and finally had to accept the fact that the pond she was standing at wasn't the lake Jymee saw looking back.

"That's okay, Wyntree," Jymee tenderly soothed the space of silence in between. "We still have our roots, and roots really are the best place to be."

Jymee watched the sun slowly set down behind the mountains, leaving a shimmering trail of pink across the lake...inviting old familiar shadowtracks to hug his heart, but in a much much bigger way.

~ Is this how you have come to love me? ~ Jymee asked his Cami-flower friend of the past ~ A pink sunset and a cute little root. How could I want anything else. ~

"Our roots," Wyntree thought as she remembered the words Jymee had left behind. Wyntree had never felt anything that close, except for Seamore and his passerbys. She could only imagine, in a sigh, what it would be like to be intertwined.

~ As for being little, it really doesn't matter what we look like topside. ~ Wyntree thought as she watched the sun say goodnight.

A soft long fine stretch of tendril and vine meandered downstream to Seamore's pond that night, where it found a place to curl around and snuggle til the light .

Jymee woke with the dawn and looked out over the lake, imagining what it would be like to somehow be the sun who kissed Wyntree's peak awake.

Downstream, Wyntree was still trying to hold on to the night. She felt so loved and snuggled and one with it all in the first touch of light. ~ This is the way I always want it to be ~ Wyntree thought, just about the time a ladybug sputtered over and landed on her top.

~ Top of the morning... ~ Wyntree faintly heard from deep down inside.

~ It's Jymee ~ Wyntree was sure. "Jymee, it that you?"

"I hope so," he said beneath the occasional gurgles. "Is anyone else playing with your root?"

"I don't think so," Wyntree replied, but she did notice a funny curled-around feeling down by her toe.

"Oh! Is that you?" she wondered on second thought.

"I don't really know," Jymee replied. "Do you feel any rocks?"

"No," Wyntree sighed.

"Then if it's tendril and vine, let it be mine," Jymee volunteered.

Amidst the gurgles and giggles, that's exactly what they decided.

Eleven

The Present ~

The meadowpatch and the woods seemed so much different now with Jymee in Wyntree's life. Funny how things can change in just one little hi.

Like a pebble tossed in a glassy pond. As it comes to rest in the soft silty bottom, it might be so wise as to know it made some ripples in it's hi, but the pond saw it change the butterfly.

"Oh my," Wyntree said to the late blooming day lily standing tall in yellow and tawny orange. "Now I know why you wanted to hide. Look how pretty you were inside."

To Wyntree, every morning woke with a smile, sunny and crisp and trimmed to the trills of the bluebird and the sparrow. The air smelled even sweeter than it did in spring, waving grasses and flopping petals in yellows and oranges and whites and pinks.

There were skips and hops and puddle-plunks and plops. Families in pairs of ducks and doves and flowers and fences and bugs. To Wyntree, everything was in love.

As Jymee was daydreaming, he remembered when he was a seedling and saw a bare little tree in the stream with only one leaf. ~I know that tree wasn't you,~ he thought of Wyntree. ~But it's still nice to dream.~

Jymee noticed some Christmas fern growing on the otherside of Seamore's bank.

"How'd you get there?" Jymee asked the clump of green-feathered wings.

Sea more
Sea
more

"Seamore? Did you do that?" Jymee asked.

~Win 'twee~gogwo~
~down strweem~

"Wyntree? Downstream? Told them to grow here?" Jymee decoded. " What am I going to do with you two?"

"Oh, let them love you, you big nut," Jo proposed.

~Love~ Jymee thought. ~We live so far apart. It might be different if we could touch tree to tree~ Jymee serenaded the breeze.

"Loving is heart to heart," came rippling back through the language of the leaves.

For awhile the pond had flowers living halfway in the water and halfway out. Some were short and squatty and some were tall and stout. The last of summer brought the pickerelweed and dandelion puffs, just in time for a visit from a black and white duck.

"Is there a lake nearby," Wyntree asked the duck between flaps and a splash.

"Upstream, over the trees," the duck replied quite naturally.

"Is there an island?"

"Big island," the duck agreed.

"And an apple tree?"

"Old grumpy apple tree," the duck was obliged to reply as he got ready to leave.

"By an oak?"

"Oak got broke," the duck flapped and quacked.

"Broke?"

Wyntree suddenly felt very sad, as she watched the duck fly east, down over the hill.

Jymee had managed to talk some flowers and nuts on his broken branch to grow.

"Seamore," Jymee said, "could you find a way to send some of my acorns downstream. I'd like Wyntree to have lots of me growing around her."

~gogwo~

~down strweem~

In the afternoon before sunset, Jymee felt a sudden sadness down in his roots. It was that same sort of sadness he remembered feeling before. Those old winter blues.

~Now what did I do?~ Jymee asked himself as he sunk down deep inside to explore. It seemed peaceful and content by the tiny cherished and snuggled lady slipper pillow.

The sadness was coming from much farther below.

As Jymee followed the feeling, he found himself at the tip of his root in Seamore's stream.

~It's not me~ Jymee realized, ~Somebody is sad downstream.~

The sadness felt like it was coming from the very place Jymee first remembered ever hearing Wyntree speak.

"Jymee?" came in a whisper that carried a familiar twinkle.

"Wyntree?" he asked. "Are you okay?"

"I saw a duck today. He told me you got broke," Wyntree said trying to keep the tears away.

"Broke?" Jymee lovingly replied. "Well, I did break a bough, but I'm fine now. It even flowered."

"How'd it happen?" Wyntree asked.

"Lightning, last spring," Jymee replied.

"Was it the big storm?"

"Yes."

"I remember," Wyntree cringed. "I felt it ...hit you."

"Hit. Me?"

"I remember the very spot in the woods."

"Then now you know where I live!" Jymee happily discovered.

"I guess...I do," Wyntree marveled as she sighed, finding herself feeling a wee bit better inside.

"I knew there had to be a reason," Jymee delighted. "You found me! That, my little Wyntree, was the gift inside all that thunder and lightning!"

The sun dipped down behind the lake, leaving a sky filled with pinks and blues and greys.

"Were you sad this past winter?" Jymee asked.

"I didn't want to live here anymore," Wyntree confessed. "I was twisted and bent and buried in snow. There weren't any flowers, anywhere."

"I felt you," Jymee said.

"You did?".

"But I didn't know it was you, until today."

One by one, the stars dusted off their sparkles in the moon's soft hello.

"Like moss is to a stone," Wyntree said, "and a butterfly is to a stem... Why can't we touch like them?"

"It's just the space our journeys need to take," Jymee tenderly tried to sooth the ache.

"But I'm with you, dear Wyntree, in the moonlight under these stars and I feel you deep down inside me. That's touching heart to heart."

Wyntree stood among the autumn afternoon's bouquet of oranges and yellows and browns, hailing to the trees, "We make a wonderful mountain of flowers."

"Don't be afraid to let go," Wyntree assured all the trees. "That's how pretty things grow."

The fall breeze that freed Jymees leaves, tickled Wyntree's needles, as it played hide'n seek up and down Seamore's stream.

And the clouds loved to peek-a-boo with the sun, dancing their shadowtracks across the treetops from lake to pond.

It was always a present to hear Thoreau and his flute echo off the lake and carol down through dell, like tying a ribbon and a bow around Seamore and the meadow.

One afternoon in the fall, another man came to the lake. He walked through the woods and found Jymee standing by the brook.

"You'll be perfect!" he declared, as he took out an axe and in a blow, started to whack.

"Uh."

chop

chop

"Why are you...

chop

CHOP!

"...cutting me?" pleaded Jymee.

chop

chop

A sick overwhelming feeling suddenly flashed through Wyntree's roots.

"Seamore!" she cried. "Seamore! In the woods! It's Jymee! Please... Please help!"

CHOP

"I'm a tree..." Jymee pleaded

chop

chop

"Not..."

chop

"...your enemy."

chop

~ a tree ~

chop

chop

~ a tree ~

Jymee drifted off to sleep.

chop

chop

Thoreau heard the chopping and came running through the woods.

chop

"What are you doing to that tree?" he shouted.

The stranger suddenly stopped, and in confusion said, "I'm... cutting it...down. Why?"

Thoreau looked at Jymee's state. It was too late. The axe was more than halfway through his trunk.

"That tree was... a friend," Thoreau said.

"I'm sorry," the man apologized. "I... I didn't know."

"I know," Thoreau sadly replied, as he tried to find a way to let go the pain.

Thoreau noticed a pink weathered ribbon laying at the base of the Jymee's tree, with one edge tucked beneath a small moss covered field stone, and the rest interlaced among a collection of mushrooms and dried nuts and twigs and leaves.

He reached down and clasped the ribbon, lifting it free to the breeze, disturbing a little salamander hiding beneath.

Standing by the edge of the stream, Thoreau watched as this strong trusted friend of the woods, dressed in all his browns and auburns for fall, was forced to break stride with the sky, like lightning to the night.

"Timber...."

Jymee's fall made a rumbling footprint down through the autumn speckled valley of oaks and birch and maples and hickorys amid a few pines,

~ ~

~

...and up to the clouds...

~

~

...as he came to lay in stillness on the ground.

A tree with many years of winter and spring in his rings... with his share of broken branches and birds nests and trails of worm holes and fungal rot from too many shady afternoons by the stream. He could have been like that elm over there on the otherside of the furrow, where a stonewall used to be. The elm that had said his last farewell years ago, it seemed... still standing there, a shell of what he used to be, home to an owl and a woodpecker and other forest beings.

As Thoreau untangled and freed the brace from among the branches of leaves, he came upon a carved heart in Jymee's bark with the words

"My Oaky."

Thoreau reached over and laid his hand on Jymee's trunk. "You're going to be okay. It's just a change," he said. "If you love these woods, you'll be back."

With his flute and the pink ribbon, Thoreau walked over to the lake shore and his canoe.

Before setting off, he turned and looked at the place where Jymee grew.

~ Someday, we'll meet again, my friend. ~

In a push, to a drift, he took up his flute and played.

It echoed softly across the lake.

~

~

~

Wyntree

Twelve

Twinkles ~

Where the meadowpatch hugged the woods, the pond sat in silent reflection. If it had any visitors, it was only in an occasional dunk or a drink at its edge.

Wyntree hadn't seen the sun for some time. Her thoughts were turned inward, down to a quiet place by her toe and the tendrilly vine.

Seamore didn't say very much. He was more peaceful now then he'd ever been. What can you say when somebody's lost their best friend?

That feeling upstream, that place where Jymee used to speak... there wasn't even a peep.

"Why are you hiding under that leaf?" Seamore asked Wyntree one fall morning as he nudged her toe.

"Leaf?" Wyntree asked.

"If you're going to flower, you need to stand tall."

"Maybe I'm not a flower," Wyntree confessed.

"Everything flowers," Seamore gently reminded her.

"And everything says good-bye," Wyntree sighed, trying hard not to cry.

"Is that how you feel, when the sun says goodnight?" Seamore reflected. "Isn't is nice, every once in awhile, to see the starry side?"

It must have been dusk or dawn, because Wyntree could hear the whippoorwill's song. As she rose and opened out into her tree, the dew told her the sun would be coming in a blink.

Mist sat on the pond, like a old familiar friend. There were leaves on the ground from trees all around. It was almost as if they'd drifted over as gifts.

Fall's gentle rays of the sun came and softly woke the wispy parting mist on the pond, as Wyntree looked down in the glassy-still reflection and saw a dainty pine.

"I guess I really am a tree," she said.

"I wish you could have seen me," Wyntree told Jymee, as an oak leaf floated down into view, turning the tree's image into tiny ripples of greens and blues.

"Twinkles don't die," Wyntree whispered to the ripples "And flowers don't hide."

Tenderly, she explored the meadowpatch and the pond. As she looked upstream, she could see a hint of Seamore's winter view, returning with the fallen leaves.

"Jymee," Wyntree called upstream, but there was only her echo in the breeze.

A crow flew over and down towards the dell. It reminded her of a lonely other-time when she thought she was the only green on the hills.

"Maybe the sky needed some of your green," Wyntree told a passing cloud as the sun set down.

The moon was half-full that night and the air crisp enough to sparkle the stars.

"In all these twinkles," Wyntree asked Jymee in the pond's reflection, "where is the twinkle we are?"

The curly-barked birch could be seen on the hill. ~ He must be married to the moon ~ Wyntree thought, ~ because he always stands out when she's here. ~

Wyntree looked up into the night, wondering how she was ever going to find a twinkle of Jymee in all that twilight.

~You'll find him in your love~

...came in a tender whisper from the birch on the hill above.

Wyntree

—ShadowTracks—

Jewel

PART III

Jewel

Thirteen

Crack ~

Winter made it's call to fall with feathery flapping flocks of geese insisting on visit ing Seamore's pond.

Honk Splash!
Honk Honk

In the sudden scurry for nuts, the forest knew it wouldn't be long before the first snow. There were nuts for the meadow mice and nuts for the crows, nuts for the quails and the wild turkeys, and nuts for the woodpeckers and the doves, nuts for the blue-jays and the raccoons and the deer, and nuts for the chipmunks and the beavers and the geese. But what about the nuts for the trees?

As the leaves fell asleep on the forest's frosty floor, Jymee's broken branches bathed in the sun where he'd once stood.

Birds still came to perch, though Jymee had lost his tree, for they saw him in all of who he was: in his roots and acorns... seedlings and twigs and leaves.

Jymee's collection of mulch was home to some ants and spiders and mushrooms and worms. Their lives hadn't changed very much, except for more sun there now than shade.

Jo felt a little out of place, standing all alone. Sure, there were trees around, but not any trees growing close. He had yellow-red stripe'd apples half-eaten and half-squished on the ground. By spring they'll probably be only leftover cores and seeds, but it won't be the same without Jymee's acorn tops and broken shells for company.

Before winter, a beaver came and mended the pond, leaving behind a baby waterfall.

Little by little, the days grew shorter, until deep in December when night was in her fullest. Wyntree stood, star-sparkled and dusted in snow, as teaberry snuggled her trunk along with an occasional mouse or mole.

Seamore's pond lay frosty frozen and chilled.

"You still have my toe," Wyntree affectionately told him, "but boy, is it cold!"

When the sun came back, Seamore's melt made a glorious crack.

CRACK#!

Time to shake the icicles free and check for buds and make ready for leaves.

Amidst all the flittering butterflies and bumble bees and ladybugs of spring, Jymee's tree lay on a hillside basking in wavy-green meadow grass speckled with clover and buttercups.

Downstream, Wyntree noticed a tiny green beginning pop up near her toe.

"You're growing awfully close to Seamore," she told the baby oak.

"If it gets too soggy," he said, "I'll hold on to your toe."

Seamore's sunlight reflection danced off Wyntree's pine.

"Seamore, are you flirting with me?" Wyntree asked, as playful ripples glittered back.

In watching the sparkles dance from bough to bough, Wyntree suddenly noticed all these baby pine cones peeking out.

"Oh, my goodness... I think I'm going to flower!"

Upstream, Seamore had overflowed. Water, water everywhere," Jo mumbled to Seamore, "Now what'd you go and do that for?"

Beneath Jymee's stump, his roots were strong and long. He still had a few knots and some clumps of crystal hanging on. Some of his roots lived in the stream, while others managed to get a tad tangled in the distant root tips of Jo and other forest underlings.

ting

tinkle

ting

"What the blazes is all that clamor" was heard down below. "Jymee? Would you please wake-up. You're rattling rocks!"

"Rocks?" Jymee replied, a little disoriented by the neighbor's fuss.

"Did you hear me?"

"Hear who?" Jymee asked.

"Don't you know me by now, or have you been blinded by the light? I'm the root of all them there yeller-red strip-ped nuts!"

"Jo?"

"Well, the Jo down below. The Jo up above only pays attention to me when he's cold."

ting

tinkle

"Would you please hush your fussing and fidgeting," Jo-below insisted of Jymee's jiggling. "It's supposed to be quiet in these parts."

"I'm sorry," Jymee hestitantly apologized, as he wondered what he'd been doing to make all that tingling. Besides, he wasn't really sure where he was anyway.

I heard him," Seamore whispered to Wyntree, as water gently lapped the lily pads.

"Heard who?" Wyntree asked, while giving her toe a bath.

"Jymee," Seamore said.

"Jymee?" Wyntree quietly questioned. "When?"

"Just now. Upstream," Seamore replied. "Where he's always been."

"But... He lost his tree."

"He's still underneath," Seamore said.

At first, Wyntree felt a little hurt and rejected. She had tried to reach out to Jymee so many times.

"I called and listened for him, but he never called back."

"He cut himself off," Seamore told her. "I don't think he knows where he's at."

He cut himself off ~ Wyntree thought, looking out through the light early evening rain.

"Dear Jymee," Wyntree prayed, "if I could only reach you some way."

As the raindrops left their shadowtracks in circles on the pond, Wyntree remembered that night under the stars, when Jymee had told her how they both touched heart-to-heart.

~ It's only the space our journeys need to take ~ she remembered him say, while she watched circles on the water gently grow from their tiny shapes.

"Why do there have to be walls in our love?" she asked, as the circles overlapped and hugged.

~ Our love. That's our love, ~ Wyntree thought as she watched the circles blend into ripples on the pond.

Across the way, Wyntree noticed raindrops perk up the leaves of the hickory tree standing by the fence.

"Just because you were cut, doesn't mean you're not loved," she told Jymee from a place deep down inside by the door of his heart.

"The rain doesn't come to take away the sun. Clouds let go the raindrops, so the raindrops can share their love.

It might be in a mist or a drizzle or a storm. But the clouds have to let go someday, so the flowers can grow."

Jewel

Fourteen

Ting Tinkle ~

Seamore tried everything he could imagine to shake Jymee awake. He yelled and poppled and gurgled and blew bubbles, but nothing seemed to work.

~noflo~ *~~*

~nogwo~

~gween

see gween~

~tor *~mo*

leen~

ting

ting

"I wish I had known about this problem before you moved in," Jo-below said to Jymee in total frustration. "This ting-tinging is making me dingy."

~noflo~

~nogwo~

ting

~mo *

leen~

*

"I'm really sorry," Jymee apologized, "I wish I could help."

ting

tinkle

In looking around, Jymee saw a crystal gem of glimmering apple green dangling off his root, winking and tinkling...

tinkle

... while another winked in pastel pink.

ting

"Where did you come from?" Jymee asked, as a third one tinged in brillant blue-green. They were enchantingly shiny little things.

ting ting

ting ting

ting

All about one of Jymee's roots dangled sprinkles of baby gems in watermelon greens and pinks.

"Where did you come from?" Jymee asked, as the pink seemed to blossom flowering feelings in colors of spring, while the green tugged at him with summer lushness when leaves touch tree to tree.

~Where did you come from?~ Jymee wondered, as he peered down deep into the rippling crystal blue green, feeling as fresh as a sunny sky, and then feeling as cold as a stream. Or was it twilight?

"Where did you come from!?" Jymee insisted of all these dangling tinkling things.

"Sometimes I wonder myself," flickered a pinpoint of light amidst the blue gem's ebbs and flows. "Can you see me?" echoed a friendly fidgety voice from somewhere inside the glow.

"See you?" Jyme asked.

"Yes. See me..." echoed back.

ting

"I'm not really sure," Jymee replied. "I think I see something. Where do you end?"

"End? I don't think I do. Do you? All I see is blue with some violet. Is that all you?"

"Me?" Jymee wondered. "I don't know. But what are you doing dangling off my roots?"

"Roots? I don't see roots."

"Is that pink crystal gem part of you, too?" Jymee inquired.

"Of course! Of course!"

"And the apple green?"

"What do you think?! Of course! Silly thing."

ting

"Do you see in pink and green too?" Jymee asked.

"When that's what I'm looking through!" the gem tingled back.

"Well, where are you now?" insisted Jymee quite perplexed.

"On the otherside of you," echoed in a bunch of tings and flickers back.

ting ting

ting ting

"The otherside of me? I'm very confused," Jymee said, as he pulled back and sat staring at his crystal companions cheerfully winking and dangling.

"A groundhog told me about you once," Jymee vaguely remembered, "but I couldn't see you then."

"That's because you were green then, nut...nut."

"Green?" Jymee asked.

"No need to be confused," the gem tingled. "I'm the meadow's jewel ."

"Jewel?"

"Every leftover leaf and nut and feather. It all gets mixed together. What did you think happens to all that stuff?"

"I guess I never thought. Mulch?"

"I'm the best of where they all got."

"Does that mean you might have some of me in there, too?" Jymee asked.

"If you're not growing green, some of you is probably in here with me."

"Can you see?" Jymee inquired.

"I only see colors: blues, greens, pinks, yellows. But you're in here somewhere. I get a little bit of everything at one time or another. That's how all this stuff stays stuck together!"

The watermelon greens and pinks tinkled and rippled and giggled.

tinkle

ting

tinkle

"Shhhh. Don't tinkle so loud," Jymee whispered. "You'll get me in trouble."

One lazy afternoon in June, Thoreau walked down a path through the woods, carrying a notepad in one hand and a flower and a twig.

"So, hows my friend?" he said, as he came upon Jymee's stump. "I thought I'd sit with you awhile and pass some time."

As Thoreau was about to settle down, he noticed a tiny green seedling peeking out of a crack in Jymee's stump.

"Well, look at that," Thoreau cheerfully remarked. "A little hickory is trying to fill your spot."

Thoreau sat next to the seedling and watched the stream wind its way down through the trees.

As he wrote, here and there a butterfly or two touched down on a leaf.

A walk through the shade of my trees to collect my leaves
and maybe a flower for your lapel or a sprig to remember me.
This road has known you well.

In a pocket, some nuts to eat and in the hand a dried branch
trusty companion to push aside a cobweb or two
or in the kick of a stone, to balance you.
This road has known you well.

A collection of wood, seasoned for the day you'd pass this way
sits bundled in your bag to make a fire for the night
friend to a book and a fine glass of wine.
This road has known you well.

And now you marry.
You've always been married, can't you tell?
This road has known you well.'

Fifteen

Sparkles ~

When the cardinal flower unfolded in all his spires of red to the hummingbirds of early morning as the ripened summer bowed her head, Jymee's tree was carried across a grass and daisy bordered path into a workshop nestled among some pines and maples and birch.

After the fall parade of browns and yellows and reds, Seamore's summer meanderings gradually appeared winding through the woods.

Wyntree was a year taller now, tall enough to see an old wooden bridge and a stone mill down in the dell.

"Dear Jymee," Wyntree said as she followed Seamore's weave upstream, "Somehow, I know you can feel me. I know, because I believe."

As Wyntree's cones opened, she noticed her seeds had wings.

"Fly to Jymee, little seeds," Wyntree whispered, as the seeds sailed away in the wind.

With the first frost, the woods and the meadowpatch bundled and boarded up and put on extra clothes. Wyntree's bark was beginning to season and peel an orangish red, a little like the birch up on the hill.

The cold brought the snow, as winter settled in. Wyntree reminded the forest to look for flower colors when they got depressed.

"They're in the icicles," Wyntree said, "and sometimes in the snow. But don't forget the blues in the sky and the oranges and reds and yellows when the sun goes by. Most of all, don't forget the sparkles. They'll make you smile inside."

Wyntree had grown to be the prettiest pine on the mountainside, the forest agreed. Seamore was so proud that he was her favorite stream.

He had jiggled and jiggled and tried to get Jymee to speak, but Jymee must have just plain decided he didn't live anymore by the stream.

"Dear Jymee," Wyntree often prayed. "How can I make you see, you're still a part of these trees."

It was a warm sunny day in December and a welcomed surprise to the woods, as Wyntree stood in all her greenness dotted with snow, watching Seamore's puddle pond enjoy a melt.

"Spring is coming," thought Wyntree's tree trunk companions, a rabbit and a mole, as one by one, the sun invited forest beings to come out from their holes.

It was fun to pretend, but Wyntree knew full well. There was still plenty more time for winter and plenty more snow.

A man walked out from the woods that afternoon, and stood by the pond. He looked around and saw Wyntree's green amidst the sparkling white.

"Aren't you pretty," he said, as he walked over and dusted her boughs. "You must get lonely living out here all by yourself. I know someone who would love to love you for Christmas. In fact, I think I'll take you home myself."

With that, he unpacked an axe and started to chop.

chop

"Uh" Wyntree said as she suddenly woke to the shock.

~ What was that?! ~ the forest gasped, as a great chill rippled up to the lake and down through the dell.

No~ ~

Ohr

What was that?

Oh! What was that?

chop Please

~Oh No!

Green

"But ..." Wyntree tried to say, as the trees called out her name.

Wyntree~

chop

Wyntree

Wyntree~

Wyntree~

Wyntree

"The meadowpatch..." ~ What about the meadowpatch? ~ Wyntree tried to say.

chop

With the last chop, Wyntree's tree fell in a bounce of softness in the snow, as the man lovingly picked her up and tied her down on his sled for the ride home.

The woods and the meadowpatch stood silent as they watched their wish-for-spring go. A sweet cedar smell followed Wyntree as her boughs brushed the sundanced snow.

~Wyn 'twee~

~Wyn 'twee~

The sled was pulled south past the pond, down over a snow-covered footpath that hugged the banks of Seamore's stream. For some, it was the first time in all their seasons of greys and browns, they'd ever seen 'the green of winter's spring'.

~Green.~

Little Green~

For them, it was a reason to believe in leaves.

The sled made its way along the footpath down through the dell, down by a mill and over an old wooden bridge where a stone cottage and a mill pond lived.

"You're going to be the prettiest Christmas tree," the man admired, as he untied Wyntree and gently leaned her upright against the shed. "I'll set you here for the night," he said, as he left.

Wyntree slowly collected her feelings as she watched a sliver of sun dip down between the trees, realizing the brook she was standing by, was Seamore's stream.

~Wyn 'twee~

"Oh, I knew you'd be here," Wyntree smiled inside at seeing her old friend.

Just being together helped the broken feelings mend.

"It's only my flower," Wyntree whispered to the breeze, asking it to touch the heart of any reaching tree. "See me in my flowers and the butterflies and the bees, if you need to see... I haven't left your heart. There I'll always be."

In the peacefulness of evening, Wyntree found herself drifting back to the place she grew, snuggled deep down in her roots.

~ You lose your leaves. I lose my stem, ~ Wyntree thought, feeling like a flower whose life had been well-spent, lying in a mossy green pillow by the water's edge.

"Dear Jymee," Wyntree softly prayed, "Please, please, know me today."

Jewel

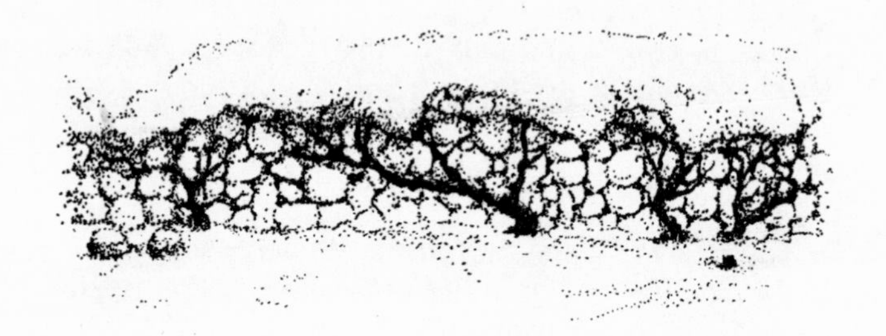

Sixteen

Dink ~

In the hush of a warm afternoon sleep, Jymee suddenly felt a rush of pain shoot down through his roots. It carried a sadness deep inside, like the biggest part of him had been torn loose.

In his memory, Jymee flashed to his tree as it broke stride with the sky. The pain of breaking, of falling... as a great weight was being lifted off his life.

Jymee's childhood lady slipper pillow welled up and spilled into a cry. ~Where are you going?~ came out in a crushed good-bye.

"It's only my flower," Jymee faintly heard, as he reached out to comfort tear drops that turned into raindrops of love. "See me in my flowers and the butterflies and the bees, if you need to see... I haven't left your heart."

The words brought Jymee back to an icey cold dusk, after a long and lonely snow.

"Cami..." quietly cried out from the shadows of his soul.

As if it were only yesterday, he could still see the lakeside glistening beneath the hills.

~ You lose your leaves. I lose my stem. ~ Jymee remembered Cami say then.

He saw her lying in the soft green moss, as Twinkitoo brushed her stem, trying to bring back her flower again.

~ My stem ~ Jymee thought, feeling achy inside. He remembered the stump of the little pine that used to live nearby.

His mind drifted to a sunset interlaced with pinks and blues and greys that carried a feeling of being married, someway.

There was a cold achiness down at the tip of one of Jymee roots. It reminded him of when he was very little and somebody very big was sitting on his shoot.

"Ouch," Jymee said as he was forced to go down and see. "Ouch! Ouch! Ouch! Who's sitting on me?!"

The achiness went away, as Jymee wiggled his root-tip awake.

~no flo~

~ *no-gwo~*

ting

"Ooh-who-who... That tickled!" trickled in a gurgle, leaving a sense of calm in its wake.

Jymee settled back down to sleep, once again feeling like everything was in its right place.

"Dear Jymee." softly knocked at the door of his heart. "Please...please, know me today."

"Today..." Jymee murmurred in a sleepy haze.

"Today..." echoed back in a sleepy way.

"But how?" Jymee dreamed.

"Like you're doing right now..."

"Now...," Jymee murmurred in a fog.

"Now?" Jymee suddenly questioned on second thought, as he peeked above his sleepy cloud. "Like I'm doing right now?"

"I never left your heart," tenderly trickled back in words that filled all the empty spots.

"Where are you, now?" Jymee affectionately asked.

"In my roots." Jymee faintly heard. "This really is my favorite place to be, with you and Seamore, underneath."

"But you do make the prettiest flower," Jymee recalled in a sweetness.

"Flowers have their season," came back in feelings that seemed to be leaving.

"Are you going? Where are you going?" Jymee reached out in his love .

"I want to spend some time with my flower."

"But you don't have to leave to do that," Jymee said.

"My flower was cut."

Jymee's heart took a crash, as a dark heavy cloud drifted over his life. ~Why?~ Jymee thought. All he could remember was the pain of his falling.

"I'm sorry," Jymee said.

"Sorry for what?"

"The pain, I remember the pain."

"But, it doesn't hurt anymore in that place."

"I wish I could hold you," Jymee said.

"You are holding me, now."

There was a tender silence, as their love intertwined, weaving through feelings that were older than time.

"Are you often out among the trees?" she asked.

"No," Jymee said. "I can't go there anymore."

"Why?"

"I'm not green."

"You were never green in the winter."

"But I was cut... too," Jymee confessed.

"That doesn't matter. You are where you love."

Jymee sat quietly with her words for awhile.

"I have to be with my flower," she said.

"Where is your flower?" Jymee asked.

"I don't know exactly. I only know that to be there, I follow my heart."

"Will you be back?"

"I never left. I live in our hug."

Jymee sat among all the memories that had found their way back into his life.

~ You are where you love. ~ He thought about that for awhile.

There was the lakeside and the stream. He loved that place. But it wasn't there anymore, at least not for him. That was another life, another time.

For a moment, Jymee saw the seedling of himself with all these tiny brown leaves sitting around the base of his tree.

~ Don't look down ~ he heard Jo say. ~ Look up. If you hadn't let go the first time, you'd still be a nut. ~

"But my tree was cut," Jymee said to himself.

An image floated through, of Twinkitoo clinging tight in the breeze to one of Cami's leaves.

~ I'll never do that again ~ Jymee heard Twinkitoo shudder.

~ Never do what? ~ Cami asked.

~ Be a cocoon ~ Twinkitoo fluttered, as he disappeared through the trees in a flittering flash of yellow.

"But I'm stuck," Jymee hopelessly cried. "I'm stuck! I'm stuck! Can't you see? I can't go back there anymore. Leave me be! Leave me be!"

Jymee locked up his feelings and sank down deep in his roots. The thought of being any place else didn't make him feel very good.

A twinkle twinked in the darkness of Jymee's roots.

*

And then twinkled again.

*

"Is that you, Jewel?" Jymee asked, but Jewel didn't clink.

The twinkle didn't really seem to twinkle, as much as it glowed, Jymee thought.

"Peek-a-boo" the twinkle-glow twinkled.

Peek-a-boo"

"Peek-a-boo?" Jymee asked.

~ Remember me?~ the tiny twinkle-glow echoed, as Jymee saw a sprinkle of twinkles in a clump with a tail. They looked a lot like his favorite meadow in the stars.

"Could that be you? Jymee asked, as he perked up.

"Dipper..." came in a giggle of recognition, as Jymee was sprinkled with love.

"Dipper..." Jymee acknowledged.

The twinkle-glow couldn't help but blush, dancing in tinkles and tickles all the way up Jymee's back.

"Where are you going?" Jymee asked in half-a-laugh.

Dipper giggled in twinkles and kept dancing, as if to coax him to stand.

"I can't go with you!" Jymee insisted to the twinkle. "I don't live up there anymore."

But the little dipper wouldn't take no for an answer, as her twinkles tickled Jymee's top.

"Now stop!" Jymee insisted. "That tickles, a lot!"

Before Jymee knew it, Dipper had tickled him up through the snow, as he found himself peering out into the hush of night, whose sleep carried the occasionally hoot of an owl and the crunch of feet against the ice.

Jymee saw Jo...with no leaves, standing old where he'd always stood dusted in snow, outlines of apples lay where they'd fallen a season ago.

"Jo..." Jymee whispered, as the sound curled about the trees standing in jagged silhouettes against the breeze.

Asleep with his dreams, Jo cleared his voice, as a little floppy-eared brown and white rabbit hopped by, leaving a trail in shadowtracks on his way to the brook.

Jymee slowly followed the rabbit's journey across the furrow where Tinystones used to live, down to the brook ambling over rocks and around clumps of snowcapped tangled twigs.

~noflo~nogwo~

~noflo~nogwo~

A dove flew over and for a moment lit on a small pine living nearby, sending an avalanche of white powder puffs trickling down her one side... down to a rise in the ground, the trunk of Jymee's tree...

~Me...~

...sitting in peaceful reflection in the lakeside's winter freeze.

```
* ~dink~    *
       * ~dink~ *

* *  ~dink~
```

A light sprinkle of snowflakes brought back tingly feelings that flowed down through Jymee's roots, dark and deep and rich with all the years of winter gleaming through.

~I've really missed this place~ Jymee sighed, as he gazed up at his little dipper friend high in the sky, twinkling to a distant flute caroling the night.

~

~

~

Jewel

Seventeen

Crackle Pop ~

Thoreau's flute played a lullabye of Christmas down through the snow-covered woods and sleepy meadows spotted with chimneys curling trails of smoke high into the moonlit and starry night, as yule logs and marshmallows were toasting inside.

At the edge of the brook, the cottage sat beneath its snowy hat with candles aglow silhouetted by frost on the windows. The front door was dressed in holly and fir, tied in a bow of shiny red ribbon with bells and pine cones.

In through the window that looked out over the brook, the woods could see their wish-for-spring in Wyntree, standing in all her green...

tinkle* twinkle*

...being gently tickled-to-wake by two ice cicles dancing in the glow of a candle playfully cheering up the brookside window.

As Wyntree looked down and around, she could see a teddy bear tucked in her boughs. He was plump and brown and a tad tattered...and very much loved.

crackle*

pOP!*

A crackle and a pop came from the last burning embers of night, cradled in the mouth of the grandfather fireplace made years ago of the stonewall by the lake.

To one side was some firewood stacked and ready to use. And on the otherside, sat a log by itself, showing all its years of growing in rings and bark with a carved heart and the words "My Oaky."

Sprigs of holly and fir draped the oak-hewn mantle where three stockings were hung, waiting for Santa and reindeer to come.

In the quiet of evening, Wyntree drifted back to her roots, leaving the sweetness of woodsmoke to cozy a teddy bear dream or two.

What was that?" Jymee asked Jewel, as a bunch of clinking and tinkling suddenly woke the crusty winter underground stillness.

"Oh, darn! There went another one," Jewel fidgeted, busily trying to bring sense to all the jiggling.

ting ~~zing

"Another what?" Jymee asked

"Star. Falling star," Jewel replied in a fuss.

"What's the matter?" Jymee asked.

"They never knock. They just zing on through and mess me all up."

"Why would they do that?" Jymee asked.

" It's their job! They're supposed to put the sparkle in all this crystally stuff," Jewel huffed.

An inviting perfume seemed to be trickling from the gem of glassy blue-green.

"Do you smell something?" Jymee asked Jewel.

"I only see colors," Jewel replied.

It reminded Jymee of the pine who used to live nearby. The day she was cut, she'd left a perfumy feeling like this in the woods. It was very inviting, but on second thought...

"I don't think I want to know anymore," Jymee decided, as his heart started to ache and feel empty inside.

"Oh, go ahead and look," Jewel told him. "It's not going to bite."

Jymee mustered up the courage, as he peered through the gem and saw some wood toasting, but that was another scent. To one side was a log with a carved heart in its bark. It seemed to have a blue-violet aura and there were the words "My Oaky." In a funny way, Jymee felt like he knew this log—intimately.

"I'm not feeling very good," Jymee said, as he sat back in his roots.

He looked again through the gem from a distance at a great fireplace made of stone. It reminded him of when he was little. It felt a lot like home.

As he looked closer, he saw two warm friendly eyes of sapphire blue that with each blink, seemed to make amber sparks in the wood's toasting. And there was a round ruby red nose with a very wide mouth below, where in a yawn, the embers glowed like moonstones.

"I think that's me, he's eating," Jymee nervously confessed to Jewel.

"Sure is mighty tasty," the fireplace named Tiny replied in a smile through the crystal.

"I don't know about these gems," Jymee said, feeling a bit queezy.

"You're just seeing where the rest of you went," Jewel informed him.

"But I think that's my tree he's eating."

"The tree you used to be," Jewel reminded him. "It might as well be a nut, now, or a leaf."

"Or maybe even mulch," Jymee added. "Isn't there anything left to me?"

"Something's got to be there," Jewel assured him, "or you wouldn't still be on the otherside of me."

Jymee gradually surrendered his feelings in the peaceful reflection of a tiny gem glimmering in pastel pink. It was the cutest little thing.

ting .

"This is much better," Jymee said, feeling relieved at the thought of whatever else he might be.

In a casual glance through the gem, Jymee noticed a wisp of pastel pink about something fuzzy and green. He felt a little sad inside. He didn't really know why.

In looking a little closer, he realized it was a pine. She had needles instead of leaves, and nuts that looked like tiny wooden trees.

ting .

The early morning sunshine played on the pine, as she wiggled a little, not quite ready to greet the light.

~ Pretty pine ~ Jymee thought to himself.

In the wisp of pink, two dreamy blue eyes appeared, looking around and down at treasures that lived there.

Two little bluebirds came to rest for a spell, on the snowcovered window box sitting outside the window.

"Meadow. Meadow" they chirped, coaxing the pine to leave.

meadow...meadow

meadow...meadow

She happily turned to see them, as her pink essence began to unfold, gently expanding and rolling out into the forest.

"Wait a minute! Wait! Please... Don't go," Jymee pleaded to the pine he'd just discovered on the otherside. "At least, not yet."

"This is not really where I live," she affectionately said, not knowing where the voice who'd just spoke to her was sitting.

"Will I see you again?" Jymee asked.

"I just want to breathe among the trees til eve," the pine whispered, as she seemed to leave on bluebirds' wings.

Jymee sat back in the gem's reflection and admired the tree.

There were all these funny inside flutterings. He didn't know why. Maybe it was because she was a tree, like he'd been once.

Maybe it was a lot of things. The feelings he felt were rich and warm and deep.

Maybe it was her glow. It had to be. All that pink.

Eighteen

Jingle ~

The cottage stirred, late morning, to a few logs tossed on the coals, and the sweet smell of hot chocolate and freshly baked cinnamon rolls.

One by one tiny trinkets of treasures were unveiled, and one by one each was dangled off Wyntree's boughs for Christmas to share.

There were silver bells and snowflakes and candy-canes and hearts...and a ball made of curly birch bark. A crocheted butterfly was hanging off one bough, and some red and yellow apples were sitting further on down. Popcorn garland was wrapped all around... and perched on one string was a dove about to sing. On the lower branch, hung a plump smiling moon sitting high above a tree-covered mountain with a tiny wooden train and a make-believe stream.

choo choo~

The finishing touch was a crystal star on the peak of Wyntree's tree. She could see the star's reflection in the window that looked out over the stream.

~A christmas tree, they called me~ Wyntree thought, as she touched back to the days of her seedling...remembering Father Winter give her a reason for being.

~ When you were only the dream of a seed, ~ he said, ~ I passed over this patch, thinking it so needed a warm fuzzy Christmas tree. And then I felt the twinkle of your love for the stream. A candlelight in the meadow. That's what you are to me. ~

One by one, presents were placed all around, as the afternoon sun peeked through the window and bathed Wyntree's boughs.

She could feel the warmth hug her needles and run down through her trunk, as she found herself following that same feeling to her roots in the meadowpatch, where her toe dangled icey cold in the pond.

"Oh!" Wyntree gasped at the shock of her icicle toe, as it popped her up out of her stump into the afternoon snow.

~ I'm really more than a stump, Wyntree discovered. ~ I still have one bough. Maybe someday, this might be a flower. ~

Jymee peered above his roots, out into the crisp evening sky, looking at the moon that, in a funny way, seemed to be smiling.

~ Some musty old feelings must have wanted to be hugged ~ Jymee thought, as he reflected on the seasons of his tree and one sultry sunset that trailed across the lake in shimmering pink.

"It's only the space our journeys need to take," Jymee remembered once saying, as a tiny door inside his heart unlocked and opened to a crack. There was more that wanted to come out, but got tangled in a tender parting from a time long past.

"Snowflakes fall," Jymee found himself singing, "and I wonder where you are... Winter's breeze echoes through the trees...

*

~It's Christmas Eve.
~It's Christmas Eve

...the stars seemed to sing.

"Night, Dipper," Jymee said to his friend in the sky, as he felt a warm fuzziness in his roots nudge him to settle down for the night.

In the quiet of evening, as all in the cottage were tucked asleep, the fire's burning embers played like a sunset sonnet to the trees.

The glow whispered ever so faintly on Wyntree's boughs, leaving feelings of being snuggled and hugged, somehow.

Reflections from some dangling snowflakes and silver bells flickered back, as Wyntree looked around at all the presents neatly stacked and wrapped.

She remembered her Christmas dream, wearing all the things she loved, as she noticed a collection of her pine cones sitting in a basket next to the Oaky log.

~This dangling moon~ Wyntree felt dancing off one bough. ~I know that's not really you. And this dove. But it is a way to remember what I love.

~I know I don't really live here. This is only my flower,~ Wyntree reflected. ~Soon it will lose its green and it won't be needing me.

~It's only the space our journeys need to take~ seemed to speak to Wyntree from the toasty embers that warmed the stonewall belly of the fireplace.

A ball dressed in curly barked birch hung off one bough. It reminded her of the otherside of spring and the birch tree's words: ~You'll find him in your love.~

A twinkling from the gem of pastel pink, seemed to flirt at Jymee in feelings that were warm and fuzzy and green.

"We never did get to touch leaf to leaf," Jymee heard whisper his way, in a blink. "But maybe that's not what's really important...being fuzzy and green."

As he followed the twinkle inside the crystal, Jymee saw those two dreamy blue eyes sitting tucked in that pretty pine, as she gazed at the embers that seemed to glisten and glitter on all the presents hanging off her boughs.

"If I could have had just one wish this Christmas eve, it would have been for you to see my tree," Wyntree dreamed. "It is the prettiest around. At least that's what the woods seem to think."

"Hmmm. Anyway, I do still have the vine," Wyntree said to the fire.

~The vine~ Jymee thought to himself in a fog of recollection. ~The vine... Isn't it supposed to be mine?~

"I never let go," Wyntree said with all the courage she could muster.

A rich warm deep forever feeling filled Jymee's roots in a far reaching hug, that rode through Seamore's frozen winter waters with a fire hot enough to make the ice crack.

~Wyntree...Could you be Wyntree?~ Jymee thought in the blush of the rush.

"Maybe Jymee is the twine...," Wyntree decided ~...that ties all these presents together.~

"I'm with you, dear Wyntree, in the stream, and in the moonlight under the stars," Jymee whispered, as he moved to caress to her boughs...

"Huh..." Wyntree gasped, in the sudden closeness of a feeling that almost made her heart stop.

"And you know? I think this is me, too," Jymee curiously discovered, as he came face-to-face with a wooden heart buried deep in her lush evergreen forest.

Wyntree suddenly felt a big wet wonderful kiss on her lips, lip-to-lip, as if a masterful snowflake had found a way to visit.

And then her eyes caught a twinkle, as two soft sultry brown eyes bashfully appeared in a blush, sitting inside a blue-violet glow, coming from a present that had two rockers and a little leather saddle and a mane and a tail...

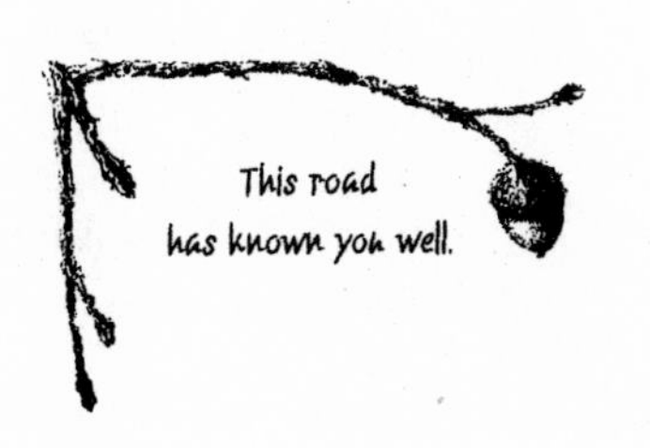
This road
has known you well.

Plickity Plunk Press, located in California's beautiful and mysterious Piute Mountains, is dedicated to making The Art of Fine Bookmaking accessible.

Developed by author Mimi Halo,
and featured in Somerset Studio magazine,
The Press offers complete hand bookbinding kits;
The BOOKMAAKER™: a complete heirloom-quality traditional bookbinding kit, and the medieval-style BOOK OF AGES™ companion kit.

"Give Your Writing The Honor
Given Every Published Work:
Bind Your Words."

Please visit us at www.plickityplunk.com